An ECLeCtIC COLLeCTIon of stuff & Things

stories by Edwina Harvey

An Eclectic Collection of Stuff & Things

stories by Edwina Harvey

edited by Simon Petrie

Peggy Bright Books

2017

First published in Australia in 2017
by Peggy Bright Books
www.peggybrightbooks.com
Please direct all enquiries to the publisher at:
editor@peggybrightbooks.com

ISBN 9780992512514

Typeset in Adobe Garamond Pro / Bolton
Cover and internal design by Simon Petrie

Thanks to Will Kenedy for additional proofreading

National Library of Australia Cataloguing-in-Publication entry

Title:	An Eclectic Collection of Stuff and Things / Edwina Harvey; Simon Petrie, editor.
ISBN:	9780992512514 (pbk.)
Subjects:	Short stories, Australian.
	Fantasy fiction, Australian.
Other Authors / Contributors:	
	Petrie, Simon, editor.
Dewey Number:	A823.4

Cover illustration by Elpis Ioannidis / Shutterstock

For Bruce

Special Thanks
to Susan Clark (Susan Batho these days),
for letting the kid have a go.

**Also by Edwina Harvey,
and published by Peggy Bright Books:**

The Whale's Tale (2009)

The Back of the Back of Beyond (2013)

Table of Contents

Introduction by Susan Batho   ix
Chippies   1
No Pets Allowed   17
Where the Last Humans Went   27
A Harem of Six Legs   29
Teach Your Children Well   43
Only Women Bleed   45
That Ain't No Emu Egg   69
Aliens Here   75
Space Cow   79
She Just Dropped In   83
Party   93
The Dragon Ring   95
HG   103
All But A Few   131
Off Course Of Course   133
'Next!' Cried the Faun   135
Everybody Wants to be St George   145
Mug   153
Divorce   163
White   167
I Saw A Man Upon The Stair   181
Earth Girls Aren't Easy   183
Vale Douglas Adams   187
Keep My Things They've Come To Take Me Home   193
When Whales Cry   203
We Were A Family Then   211
Writes of Passage   213
Biography in a Tea Cup   217

If you're looking at the table of contents and thinking, "I've read all of these", chances are you haven't. A few of the offerings here haven't been published before, and I'm a real fiddler when it comes to writing. I find I'm always tweaking things, changing things around whenever I review anything I've written. This book was no exception.

Introduction

Edwina Harvey has always been a writer and science fiction enthusiast. I suspect she was born with inky hands, from trying to write *in utero*, but only the delivering doctor would know for sure. She has always been a writer. All writers would know what I mean. I met Edwina as a young teenager (whilst she still knew everything) when she had formed a Star Trek club with her friend, Julie Townsend. They both came up to our Mountains home, and strong friendships were formed, along with a merging of clubs to create ASTREX. I was already editing fanzines at that stage and got to read, and in some cases edit, some of her early fantasy work. Her dragon stories were my son's favourite reading. The rest is history, of course. She is the author of one of my favourite young adult novels, *The Whale's Tale*, one of my favourite hucksters— always recommending a new author, selling great books and merchandise. I am really looking forward to this one.

Susan Batho
4th May, 2017

Chippies

In the way that strangers do, he did his best to ignore the woman who sat two seats along from him in the half-empty bar. He'd taken in her long, slender form in a cursory glance when he scanned the bar for a seat as he first walked in. Once seated, a surreptitious look had told him that she was drinking a cocktail complete with bits of fruit and paper umbrella decorating the top of the glass.

Sure she was nice enough to look at, conservatively dressed with shoulder-length black hair and a curvaceous figure, but he was more interested in a couple of beers to take his mind off his working day before he headed home. He was troubled by his conscience.

He always drank wine at the corporate functions. It was expected. He even managed to appear knowledgeable about what he drank. He drank wine when colleagues socialised as well. Drank where they drank, ate what they ate. This bar wasn't in that league, nor in that neighbourhood. He could enjoy a few beers here safe in the knowledge that he wouldn't be recognised, not sneered at for drinking what he wanted to instead of fitting in with all the rest.

There was a television over the bar. The news was on. The bar patrons' eyes all gravitated to the images that were broadcast, as people do when they're keen for something to hold their attention.

A short item appeared about a man who had died on a busy city street in front of plenty of witnesses. They all said his body had just ignited then been engulfed by flames. There were images of his charred remains, not that there were any left to speak of, just some soot, ashes and his pair of shoes seemingly unscathed.

The woman with the cocktail gave a nervous laugh. Embarrassed by the stares of her fellow drinkers, she cast her eyes back to her glass and took a large gulp of her drink as if to steady her nerves. She seemed agitated about something. From the corner of his eye he thought he saw her shiver.

On the TV the news broadcaster was saying it was the fifth case of what appeared to be spontaneous combustion to occur in the city in a month.

"Yeah, right," the woman muttered, draining her glass and making a meal of the fruit decoration.

He decided this was an opening line, or about as close as it was going to get. He got off his bar stool and moved to the one next to hers.

In the time-honoured tradition of bar-users everywhere when endeavouring to start a conversation, friendship or something more, he offered: "Can I buy you a drink?"

She regarded him with a grin that suggested she was about to refuse. But then she must have reconsidered because her smile grew wider and she acquiesced. "Sure, why not?"

He got the bartender's attention and ordered the same again for them both.

"My name's Harry by the way," he said, deciding that if they were going to talk there wasn't going to be anonymity. He extended his hand to her.

"Selina," she replied. Shaking the proffered hand firmly, assessing him both by touch and a look that seemed to devour him.

"So, what was so amusing about that newscast?" he asked.

The drinks were set before them and there was a brief interlude as Harry reached into his suit pocket to pay for them.

She seemed suddenly shy, playing with the paper umbrella in her fresh cocktail. "Oh, spontaneous combustion."

"Spontaneous combustion amuses you?"

She looked him straight in the eye. "People being gullible enough to believe it amuses me—or rather it disturbs me."

"I thought there'd been cases of it in the past?"

"Oh yes, well documented cases. All unexplained but scattered through time and in different countries. Certainly never five in one city in one month. And considerably more around the country in that same time frame."

"What?"

"Oh yes. There's been a growing trend for these 'spontaneous combustions' in the past year all around the world."

"How do you know?" Harry reappraised her. She was obviously more than the bank or office worker he'd originally taken her for.

"I've been following the cases, Harry. They're of personal interest to me. Nice suit you're wearing by the way. Where do you work?"

"I'm in banking," he replied, curious at her sudden diversion.

"I'm a doctor," Selina informed him before he could ask, and her answer surprised him. You didn't usually find doctors swilling lavish cocktails in bars in this part of town. "Or at least I was before I was struck off."

This surprised him even more. "What for?" he asked before he thought better of it, though he suspected he already knew the answer. But it wasn't very diplomatic of him, and he didn't mean to pry.

"For immunising my little girl."

"Doesn't sound like any crime to me," Harry replied with a shrug. Not the answer he'd been expecting. He took a sip of his beer.

"No, it doesn't, does it? Not unless you know a bit about what is going on behind the scenes," Selina stated, making it obvious she thought she knew some hidden agenda.

It piqued Harry's curiosity. "Are you sworn to secrecy?"

She laughed again, quietly this time so as not to draw attention to herself; but warmly, as if she was prepared to share the secret. "Ah, Harry, where to begin …? Tell me, are you married?"

"No."

"So you have no children?"

"Not that I'm aware of." Her abrupt changes in subject disturbed him a little.

"Were you immunised as a child?"

There she went again. But he had to think about this one. He dimly remembered visits to the doctors, needles, crying afterwards, but his mother had always been proud of the fact that she'd kept his protection up to date. He found himself nodding, though he was puzzled as to where her questions were leading.

"Were you ever taught how, about 30 years ago, world governments had *really* started a push for every child to be immunised? It had been a big issue before, or course, but then immunisation became compulsory. Now, why do you think that was?"

"World health, I suppose," Harry replied. "To stop children dying of measles, fight the re-emergence of whopping cough, polio, that sort of thing. Hadn't there been a swing away from immunisation that saw a lot of the previously eradicated diseases reintroduced prior to that?"

"Yes there had, but not for the reasons you think. Most of those who were anti-immunisation cited live viruses and the chance of serious side-effects as their reasons not to have their children immunised. At least at first. Then a growing number from the medical and scientific communities thought about not immunising their kids—or at least not taking them to government-run hospitals or clinics to be immunised. Most either immunised them themselves, or went to people they trusted to get them immunised privately. But the governments didn't like that, so they started crackdowns and purges. If you didn't have a certificate from one of the recognised immunisation clinics, your life was stuffed. You'd know that yourself."

"Yes," he concurred, recalling how a proper immunisation certificate was a vital form of ID these days, even for ensuring things like a housing loan from a bank.

"It's never bothered you?" Selina probed.

Harry took a swig of his beer, stared thoughtfully into the glass and realised it never *had* bothered him. Now he wondered why people applying for a loan had to produce their immunisation certificate before the loan could be approved.

Because if they got sick and died you'd lose the loan …? No, you'd just repossess their property. Or was it that if they got sick they'd infect all their neighbours? No, because presumably the neighbours were immunised and thus protected from the disease.

"Ah," Selina commented on his protracted silence. "It seems to be bothering you now."

"I never really thought about it before," Harry confessed.

"Why should you. Harry? Why should any of us? It's easier to just do as we're told."

She sipped her flamboyant cocktail, the potent liquid seemingly making her more talkative. "You ever have a dog, Harry?"

"Sure, when I was a kid." Harry shrugged, fondly remembering the death row special from the pound he'd been given for his eleventh birthday. "No pedigree or anything. Just a mutt. But as bright and as faithful as they come."

"I bet he had been microchipped when you got him."

"Yeah, I remember being grateful that he had been. That way I knew if he ever ran away from home he'd be found and returned to us. Not that he ever wandered though."

Selina took another sip from her drink, glancing around the bar to see if anyone was paying attention to their conversation before lowering her voice conspiratorially. "They tested the technology on animals first, Harry. Then they progressed to human subjects, mostly soldiers when they joined up."

"You're joking!" Harry laughed loudly then felt embarrassed at breaching the peace at the bar.

"Go look it up, Harry. It's still in the public records. Israel led the way, then other countries where military service was mandatory. Soon just about every country in the world was doing it; a little after taking a soldier's DNA sample became fashionable. You know, so they could positively identify the body when there wasn't much body left to identify."

"Why?"

"For a banker you're not too quick on the uptake, are you? So they can trace their soldiers using satellites. A squadron gets lost behind enemy lines, they can be directed back to safety; a soldier gets taken hostage, they know exactly where he is and can plan to get him out."

Harry looked at her in stunned disbelief. He suspected he knew where this scenario was going and he didn't like the conclusions he was forming. His voice dropped as low as hers. "You mean you're trying to tell me the next step was to secretly microchip everyone? That's why immunisation programs became compulsory?"

Selina nodded, took another sip from her glass. "Simple, isn't it?"

Too simple! Harry struggled *not* to believe what she'd just confronted him with, but all the pieces added together made a frightening picture. Except for spontaneous combustion. He wasn't sure he completely understood that bit.

"I've got a friend who worked in a crematorium," Selina informed him. "I know it takes pretty intense heat to incinerate a body to ash. I doubt those people 'self-combusted', at least not without a lot of help, at any rate."

"Help from where?" Harry wanted to know, his voice barely a whisper.

"Harry, our satellites have the ability to read a number plate on a car going through a red light. If they can lock in on a number plate then they can lock on to a human being. If they have cameras installed in them, why not laser weapons or microwave generators?"

"Stop!" Harry said. "It's too much. I don't want to hear the rest."

Selina shrugged. "Suit yourself. You're just like everyone else. The truth is hidden in the most obvious places. It's right there in front of you. Just no one wants to believe it. Well, not many at any rate."

"But why? Why would a government elected by the people wilfully commit murder on innocent victims and make it look like some freak of nature?"

"Innocent victims, Harry? If you bother to delve into the history of the victims you'll find that they are drug runners, terrorists, tax cheats, embezzlers, or they've accrued a mass of unpaid parking fines …"

Parking fines? Harry got the idea that Selina could have kept going. He felt himself break into a cold sweat, though he thought she'd been trying to lighten things up when she said parking fines.

"It's probably very humane," she assured him, aware of his nervousness. "I doubt they know what's going on. Maybe they just get a hot tingly feeling, then it's goodbye cruel world. They wouldn't *know* they were about to die—but then neither do unwanted pets before they're put to sleep."

Harry looked at her strangely.

"Sorry," she apologised with another shrug. "I work as a vet's assistant. It was the closest I could get to human medicine once they stopped me practicing as a doctor."

"And your little girl?" Harry asked.

"They made sure she was chipped, then they put her in a foster home. I'm denied all access. I think if I tried to see her *I'd* probably self-combust. That guy who we saw on the news—I was supposed to meet him here, take him back to where I work and remove his chip. I'm part of an underground we've got going …"

With anxious gulps Harry drained his glass of beer. The conversation with Selina had unnerved him and he wanted to get out of the bar as quick as he could. It was as if someone had pointed out that the sky was green after he'd accepted—believed—that it was blue all his life. It was all too frightening and he wanted to ignore it rather than accept that maybe it was real.

"It's been nice talking to you," Harry said hurriedly, his words almost tripping over themselves in his haste.

"Oh, you're leaving now? Well, thanks for the drink." She seemed nonplussed by his agitation and she smiled warmly as he got off his bar stool, smoothed his elegant suit and exited the bar.

He tried to calm down as he walked briskly away from the bar. He'd never noticed her there before, it was likely he'd never see her in there again. But just in case, the next time he fancied a couple of beers and quiet reflection before heading home he'd find another watering hole.

In the next two days he did his best to forget all that Selina had told him, but his mind kept coming back to it again and again.

He had to give her credit as a storyteller. He was a mature man who didn't get off on horror stories, but her little tale had got right under his skin and it just kept crawling around making him *damned* uncomfortable.

An urban myth; surely nothing more? But the story of the crocodile in the sewers and the maniac killer on the highway didn't rattle his psyche the way Selina's story did.

Without intending to, he found himself trawling the net, looking up articles on microchipped pets and soldiers. It seemed Selina had her facts right, though not surprisingly, he couldn't find any information about the global population being chipped.

If he had a clear conscience it mightn't have unnerved him, but he kept thinking again and again of that cleaner program he kept secretly running through clients' accounts at the bank where he worked. It was almost expected that when one reached his level of management they'd have some sort of scam running to ensure a happy early retirement. His program wasn't greedy; it would irregularly sweep through all the accounts deducting seventy cents from each. An amount that small could easily be ignored by most account holders, and if anyone commented on it they were usually told by Customer Services that it was a balance error, or an increase in charges.

Harry knew he was one of many in banking management using the system for his own benefit in this way. Occasionally someone would get a little greedy or careless and get caught.

But mostly the rest went on squirrelling money away into their special accounts unnoticed.

Still Harry was unnerved. He began to worry that someone was watching him and he knew now that he couldn't run or hide if they blew the whistle. Getting to sleep each night wasn't as easy as it had been a week before.

A clear sunny day a few days later saw Harry choosing to eat his lunch in the nearby central city park. He waved at his work colleague, Mark, as the man went jogging by. Mark was on the same management level as Harry, but keen to keep climbing the corporate ladder, hence his image of keeping fit.

There was an odd buzz around the bank Harry noticed as soon as he returned from lunch. There seemed to be more conversations going on than usual and a sense of agitation in the air. Excitement wouldn't have described it adequately. It was only when he'd taken the elevator to his floor that he found out what had everyone talking.

"Incredible about Mark, isn't it?" Alicia said in passing, presuming Harry had already heard.

"What happened?" Harry asked.

"Apparently he just exploded into flames."

Harry felt the blood rush from his face and his hands went clammy at this news.

"He what?"

"Madison witnessed it. He was just jogging up the hill towards the bank one minute and the next minute he was engulfed in flames. They've cordoned off the side-street. The police are still down there; don't know about the ambulance officers. There wasn't a lot left of him when they got there apparently."

Harry bolted for the elevator, leaving a confused Alicia in his wake. He didn't want to believe what he'd just heard, but was determined to see the evidence with his own eyes. As Alicia had said, the police had roped off the area with blue and white striped tape. He could smell burnt meat on the breeze and he could see ominous scorch patches on the stone wall of the building as well as on the footpath. A policeman was carefully picking up what was left of a singed pair of state of the art runners. Harry felt sick. He knew Mark had a bigger, better collection program 'vacuuming' his clients' accounts, he had intimated as much to Harry more than once and he hadn't been too concerned about covering his tracks.

Someone, somewhere had been watching; had known what Mark was up to and had ensured he was taken out of the game.

Harry realised everything Selina had told him must have been true. He had proof of it here, right before his very eyes. A policeman looked like he was about to ask Harry if he had any business being here, or to move on, but Harry turned away before he had the chance, and staggered back into the bank, pale and shocked.

He worked like an automaton through the afternoon. Only one thing kept running through his mind: he had to find the Underground that Selina had told him about and get himself de-chipped. Ideally he had to locate Selina again.

Time dragged its heels that afternoon while Harry waited anxiously for the day to be over so he could pursue his own interests and not the company's. When it was finally a decent hour to leave the workplace without raising eyebrows (who could blame anyone for not wanting to work back after what had happened to Mark today?), Harry bolted from his office like a man with a bomb attached to his back, conscious that it could go off at any moment without warning.

He headed back to that bar where he'd first encountered Selina and the truth a few days before. She wasn't there and he almost decided to head for home when logic took control of his maddened thoughts. He'd never find her if he went home. But if he sat at the bar and waited, maybe even asked a few questions of the bartender or the other regular drinkers, then perhaps he would at least find a lead.

Breathing deep controlled breaths Harry crossed to the bar, sat down and ordered a beer. In four grateful gulps he managed to drain his glass so he ordered another, determined to take his time drinking the second one at least.

It was still early and the bar seemed thinly populated. She might turn up later if she was going to turn up at all. He tried to remain optimistic. He was nearly to the dregs of his second glass of beer when she eased herself onto the bar stool next to his.

"Hiya, Harry. I was hoping to see you here." She seemed genuinely pleased to see him.

"Selina!" He made her name sound like a sigh of relief. "Can I buy you a drink?"

She nodded and signalled the bartender. He brought her a glass of white wine without being told what sort she wanted, proving to Harry that he'd been on the right track; she was a regular here. That she wasn't drinking a frilly multi-layered cocktail this time somehow conveyed that the tone of their relationship had shifted. This was serious business.

"You've got to help me," Harry cut to the chase. "A guy I work with went up in smoke at lunch time."

Selina frowned, taking a measured sip from her glass. "A lot of unusual phenomena been going on," she replied casually, glancing around the bar, looking for anyone who might be taking an interest in their conversation.

"I've got to get rid of this thing," he whispered urgently to her. "Before I end up barbequed too."

"Sure, I could do that for you. But there'd be a charge."

"How much? Just tell me," Harry said as if money was no object. It wasn't when it was someone else's money he intended using.

"Thirty thousand."

"Not a problem."

Selina picked up a drink coaster, produced a pen from her handbag and wrote a series of numbers on the coaster. To the casual observer she might have been giving him her phone number.

"I'm with the Midwest banking group. This is my account number. Make sure the money's deposited by noon tomorrow. Here's my number in case you need to call me. Otherwise, I'll meet you here tomorrow evening, say 5.30?"

"Sure," Harry said with a smile, carrying on the pretence that they'd just hooked up for a date as he pocketed the coaster.

It went off as arranged. Harry scraped $30,000 painlessly out of other people's accounts, a few cents here and there so he wouldn't get noticed. He made sure the funds were transferred to her well before noon. He'd toyed with the idea of artificially creating a deposit in Selina's account, but that was too risky and could be traced back to him if discovered.

Harry had spent most of the previous night lying awake scheming what he could get up to once he was assured he was a free man. He was angry that 'the powers that be' had played with the rights and freedoms of individuals, secretly invoking justice when and where it suited them. He planned on creating funds for the freedom fighters when all this was through, it would be his way of helping the Underground.

Selina turned up at the bar at the pre-arranged time. Harry noted that she appeared nervous, but figured that might be natural. He was feeling a little edgy too.

"Shall we go?" he asked.

"How about a drink first? To steady my nerves—and yours. You could probably do with some muscle relaxant."

"Sure," Harry acquiesced.

He ordered a beer for himself while Selina ordered a shot of vodka which, much to Harry's surprise, she downed in a single gulp, banging her shot glass on the bar when she'd drained it. He recalled how she'd dithered over her cocktail on the night they'd first met. Now, by comparison, he dawdled over his beer, taking time out for small talk which seemed to annoy her.

"I'm sorry," he said, having finally drained his glass. "I get chatty when I'm nervous."

He wondered, as they paid for their drinks then left the bar, if anyone had noticed them and what had been made of them if they'd been observed? Hopefully they looked no more sinister than a couple on their first date.

Within ten minutes Harry stood in the back room of an inner-city veterinary clinic. He was surrounded by cages in which a variety of dogs slept, yapped, barked or watched him with interest.

The cats and other animals, he'd been informed, were housed in another room.

Having asked him to remove his coat and shirt, Selina had proceeded to run a concave dome over his left arm. It bleeped suddenly, making him jump. She looked up at him with a calming smile on her face. "Found it. Now for the gruesome part."

She applied a topical anaesthetic swab and deftly cut an 'X' into his upper arm with a scalpel. A little probing with a pair of forceps and she had it.

"Voilà!" she announced, showing him a microscopic piece of metal on the tip of the forceps.

"That's it?" he asked as she put the chip down and bandaged his arm.

"Of course. That's your identity."

"What will you do with it now?" he asked.

"Oh, I'll ask for a volunteer." She glanced meaningfully around the room. "That way if they check up on you you'll appear to be still moving, though they'll wonder at the change of address and other patterns. Or I could just destroy it if you prefer."

"That sounds like the best option, I think," Harry replied, not wanting to condemn any dog to death for his misdemeanours.

"You'll probably start getting vaccination reminder messages if I do that. Doctors you visit might suggest you get a whooping cough or tetanus booster shot, or maybe a flu vax needle. But I'm sure you'll be able to work your way around those."

"I can't thank you enough," Harry said as he slipped his shirt and coat back on.

"It was my pleasure," Selina replied. "Are you ready to go?"

She showed him through to the back lane they'd used to gain access to the clinic. He didn't notice the four men loitering, hidden in the shadows of the alleyway, he was too overcome with relief that the authorities could no longer touch him, control his life, sanction his death remotely.

They were on him before he knew it. He didn't even have time to cry out as they efficiently silenced him and carried his slumped body away. One figure, the leader of the four, offered a salute to Selina who stood in the open back doorway preparing to leave.

She nodded, shut the door behind her then wrapped her arms tightly around herself. The night had grown cold all of a sudden.

Others would come soon, she knew. They'd bring charred remains of Harry's clothes with them and they'd leave soot and scorch marks on the white-washed walls and on the path. Harry's demise would make tomorrow's news. Five minutes of fame as an unnatural phenomenon. And Selina would have another $30,000 bounty in her bank.

When 'Chippies' was finally published in Aurealis, *Issue 19, 1997, I did the happy 'They just published my story!' dance all writers do. I showed my friends, I showed my colleagues, I showed my father (who had vision problems, but was still able to read the newspaper in good light at that stage). "Can you see who wrote this?" I asked him gleefully. "Can you see my name there?" "No," he responded, peering at the page where my name appeared in fairly large print. At first I was despondent, but then the gloves came off. He'd unwittingly liberated me. I could write what I liked without fearing he'd read it.*

I'd submitted many stories to Aurealis *prior to 'Chippies' without any luck, but felt I was getting closer.* Aurealis *tended to publish dark fiction, so my submissions to them got darker and darker until they finally accepted 'Chippies'. I'd broken through the 'dark ceiling'.*

No Pets Allowed

Sure I'll tell you about my last flatmate.

He's one of those role-playing sorts. You know, plastic models on every non-moving square inch of furniture, replica guns in his underwear drawer (not that I look in his underwear drawer all that often, you understand). Posters of nuclear-powered beach buggies on most of the walls, a poster of the cast from the Big Bang Theory plastered to the ceiling. Not that unusual really.

Me? Well, I'm more the science-fiction/fantasy type. With a pet unicorn. How imaginary the unicorn is depends on how pure your heart is, and whether or not you have ever been startled awake in the middle of a dream in the middle of the night to find the business end of a horn poised at that delicate space between your eyes.

He likes chocolate and ice-cream a lot, that unicorn. Life got a lot easier when I got a flatmate who accepted that it wasn't *me* eating all the chocolate and ice-cream. Okay, so life got a little easier when I taught the unicorn how to open the fridge door too.

You allergic to unicorns by any chance? You allergic to any equines as far as you know? No, no reason for asking …

I had a cat not that long ago, too; and I want to get another one pretty soon to fill the void, but I'll tell you more about that later.

Ah, my last flatmate! Bean he was known as. Has Bean, Bean There Done That, Bean Too Long. I've got loads more. It's not the sort of name you can take seriously, can you?

And he had some strange friends. They'd come over and they'd spend the whole night either talking in his room about role-playing things like fourteenth level dungeons, thirteen-sided dice, Klingon battle cruisers and salvos. (No, not the op-shop where you can buy cheap clothes and those round things music was stored on before downloads were invented. Records! Yeah, them.)

When they weren't in his room talking about things I know nothing about, they'd be in the lounge room playing these games, usually while they were drinking cocktails containing certain substances that weren't quite legal. That didn't really worry me, because if they were sipping on their cocktails it meant they weren't drinking *my* Coca-Cola. Any person of high social standing should have a fridge stocked with the real thing. And I work nightshifts and weekends, so I need it for medicinal purposes and reckon it should be tax-deductable.

I don't take kindly to any freeloaders helping themselves to my collection of Coke, though the unicorn is exempt from this ruling. He likes a can on hot summer nights, especially when he's been up at the racecourse pretending he's winning the Melbourne Cup.

When Bean was alone (which wasn't very often, because after a while all his friends became dependent on his cocktails), he dabbled in magic. That's okay with me, because I'm pretty tolerant of anyone's religion. He used to walk around the flat naked chanting incantations too, but that didn't worry me either because he hasn't got anything I haven't seen on a centrefold in Cleo or Playgirl. (No, I wouldn't dream of looking up that sort of thing on the net—well, at least not when the boss was passing through the office.)

What I didn't like about Bean's practices were that they'd upset my stomach. One of our few differences of opinion was that I could have a psychic stomach that was sensitive to magic.

I—as the owner of the stomach—claimed it was true. Bean, on the other hand, was always of the opinion that I did too much overtime at work to pay for my dependency on Coca-Cola, and the caffeine and stress combined were no doubt giving me an ulcer.

Apart from upsetting my stomach, I can't be sure how effective his occult-ish dabbles were. We live in one of those suburbs where break and enter is pretty common, so Bean thought it would be prudent to lay a 'Thief deterrent spell'. I thought it must have been powerful because I had to break out the Alka-Seltzer. Bean just sniffed and told me it served me right for working both days of the weekend.

His spell worked really well. We were robbed the next day. They got my TV, my DVD player and iPad, but they didn't touch any of the junk in Bean's room. (No doubt not much call for a Commodore 64 computer you're hanging on to to sell as an antique any day now, and they didn't see the value of an old Betamax video recorder either. The 13 sided dice, Cthulhu prints and drawer of miniature military figurines were likewise overlooked.) Bean claimed this proved his spell had worked. I said it only proved the thieves were after stuff they could fence before they got too hot, though it also proved I don't spend all my overtime on Coca-Cola. We were both right, no doubt.

If Bean had any redeeming characteristics (apart from being able to unblock a sink and put the garbage out) it was his thing for dragons. I liked his vast knowledge of dragon lore. I liked his models, posters and books of them, but most of all I loved the way his eyes lit up with enthusiasm when he talked about them. He could, and would, talk the night away until dawn just telling you about dragons.

I came home one night after working back late, my arms all but dragged out of my sockets by the four bottles of 2 litre Coke (hey, they were on special!) cradled in those supermarket plastic shopping bags that were designed by a sadomasochist to rip through your fingers if you tried to carry home more than 100 grams of feathers in them. Yes, I know, I should have been using my canvas shopping bags, and most of the time I do, but the special caught me unawares, so don't guilt me out, okay?

I'd had a hard day at work, I was tired, my knuckles were dragging on the floor by this stage, and all I really wanted was a nice hot bath, a refreshing glass of Coke and to crawl off into bed with my favourite author ... or at least his most recent book.

I dumped the Coke in the fridge, grabbed a few squares of chocolate hoping that the unicorn wouldn't notice them missing, then headed to the bathroom, put the plug in the bath and turned on the taps.

That's when I saw it and screamed.

"Bean!"

"Hmmmm?" It was the same non-committal noise he makes when I've seen a humungous spider and want him to deal with it.

"What the hell is this thing in the bath?"

"What thing?"

"This big thing."

"Oh *that* thing. It's mine. I got it today."

"Well, would you mind removing it?"

"It's alright where it is. You just go ahead and have your bath. It won't bother you."

Won't bother me? How could something that was spherical, dirty looking and almost half my height *not* bother me? Granted, if it had been wrapped in foil I would have mistaken it for the largest Easter egg I've ever seen, and probably wouldn't have been so bothered, but the fact of the matter was that it was sitting in the middle of the bath tub where I had intended to take a bath, and the hot water I was going to use to soothe away my tensions was swirling around it.

You know the cost of water these days. The overtime didn't just buy toys and Coca-Cola. I really wanted to soak in some steaming hot water right now. I doubted I could move the newest bathtub fixture without rupturing a disc or giving myself a hernia (*Damn it! Why couldn't Bean just get himself a rubber duck like everybody else?*), and I didn't want to send all that lovely hot water gurgling down the sink without giving me some benefit first. So I got out of my clothes and into the bath, carefully arranging my legs around the great lump of a thing in the middle.

"Bean!" I shouted my displeasure through the door. "Bring me a Coke!"

Bean knows enough about women to know that once a month they need a slave. A large glass filled with my favourite beverage was at the end of a familiar arm inserted through the door while he carefully gazed in the opposite direction.

"Thank you." Just because I treat him like a personal servant doesn't mean I can't be polite.

The arm was removed, the door was dutifully closed behind, and I was once again serene in my steamy haven, except for the frown when I contemplated the boulder I shared the bath with. There was something not quite right about it ... was that noise coming from it, or was that the old lady upstairs practicing her tap-dancing again? (I think she uses real taps!) And was that thing rocking, or what?

When I heard and saw the cracks appear, my caffeine oversaturated system had me up and out of that bath at the speed of light, wrapping a bath sheet around me as a reptilian head emerged from the shell and I stared into the face of a newborn baby dragon.

"Bean, get in here NOW!" I hollered in my best Nefertiti, Queen of the Nile impersonation.

"Gee, you drank that Coke quick," Bean informed me, arriving at the bathroom door, Coke bottle in hand.

He wasn't expecting the bathroom door to be flung open for him, he wasn't expecting to see me wrapped in a towel. He may have thought all his Christmases had come at once, but then he looked past me at the big lizard with wings emerging from its shell and fell hopelessly in love.

"My baby! The hot water must have stimulated the hatching! I'll just clean him up and you can get back in the bath if you want."

I glanced into the bath. Get in and soak in all that amniotic fluid? I don't think so.

The dragonling made a "peep peep" noise. I think it was bonding with Bean.

"Well, congratulations, Daddy." I doubt Bean heard the sarcasm in my voice. He was too busy breaking off parts of shell, and wiping the hatchling down with one of the towels.

"I wasn't expecting you so soon! You must be hungry. What have we got to feed you?"

"We've got chocolate," I informed him.

"Or maybe you need a liquid diet first?"

"We've got Coke." Yeah, I'm just Little Miss Helpful, aren't I? "You'd better go to the convenience store and get some milk or something."

Typical man! He was totally unprepared for motherhood.

It was the first time I saw Bean flustered. He was torn between being the Mother-Nurturer and the Hunter-Gatherer.

"I'll keep an eye on the little fellow. You go get him something to eat and drink. Now go! But take the canvas bags! I've already tried to ruin the planet today. Don't you come home with plastic bags!"

I don't think he ever heard me. Bean went faster than I'd ever seen him move before, while I sat on the toilet seat and admired the newborn dragon, who I had to admit was kind of cute, especially with those hypnotizing amber eyes.

Bean was back before I knew it, ushering me away from his dragon. (*Oh, these clucky boys!*) He'd bought four litres of milk and a box of hamburger patties. That would have worked as a first meal, I guessed.

I went off to put on some clothes, but not before the unicorn wandered in and sniffed warily at the baby dragon before heading for the fridge and the chocolate. He obviously wasn't too happy about the new arrival, because he went out to air his grievances to the cat. I can't say I blame him.

I considered my own situation: now I shared a two-bedroom middle storey flat with a role-player, a cat, a unicorn and a baby dragon … I wondered how we'd all get along.

I didn't have to wonder for long.

For the first few days it was no big deal; I just stepped around the dragon do's and puddles. It was Bean's dragon, Bean could clean up after it. And he did, providing I yelled and tantrummed enough to motivate him.

But flight and fire come early to dragons. Once it started shooting flames and exercising its wings things got a little out of hand.

The dragon got peckish one night and char-broiled the cat, which put my relationship with dragon and Bean (not to mention the ghost of the deceased cat) on edge. I was fond of that cat. That cat had been like a cat to me. I'd raised it from a kitten. Without the cat, the unicorn only had me to talk to, and it seemed to think my conversations—revolving as they did around how much I hated my job and how much I enjoyed chocolate and Coca-Cola—were substandard. The unicorn had never considered Bean worthy of conversation, and that wasn't likely to change now the flat had been turned into a baby dragon crèche.

But it didn't stay a baby dragon for long. The damn thing grew faster than anything has a right to.

When Bean's bedroom could no longer accommodate dragon and Bean, Bean started sleeping on the lounge. But the lounge isn't that comfortable, and that arrangement only lasted a few nights.

I should point out that Bean's gamer friends came over, saw the dragon (how could you miss it?) and all swore off drinking his cocktails with the illegal ingredients. He didn't see them again, but he didn't really miss them, because he had more important things on his mind.

The garage downstairs would be a good place for the dragon to live, Bean decided, his back in agony from sleeping on the lounge by this stage. So my car got evicted, set free to roam the street ... okay, I had to park it half a block away, but you get my meaning.

Getting the dragon out of the flat, down the stairs and into the garage without any nosey neighbours catching us was a logistics nightmare, but somehow we managed.

And that was fine for a while. Only it was still growing, and our fun wasn't over yet. When the dragon had got to the stage where its wings scraped the walls of the garage, he ... err ... sort of got out one day. Turns out, unlike bats and bank customers, dragons aren't particularly happy about being left in the dark all of the time. No doubt he craved the wild blue yonder, the wide open spaces. Truth to tell, Bean had been a bit slack cleaning out the newly appointed dragon barn and the poor thing was probably keen for a breath of fresh air as well. It can't be much fun breathing in the heady odour of your own excrement, I'm sure.

There was no way I was letting Bean drive my car, so he played sky-searching navigator while we chased his dragon around various suburbs. The damn thing tried to pick off a couple of German shepherds along the way. I bet they'll be seeing the doggy psychiatrist for some time to come.

I guess we were lucky that this was the dragon's first flight. It soon got tired and landed in a park, where Bean cornered him. I sort of kept my distance … I mean we got along okay this dragon and I, and I didn't want to spoil the relationship by telling it that it had been a very, very naughty boy.

Best to leave that to Daddy.

So Bean made a dragon-halter out of a bundle or rope he'd thrown in the car. Then he leaped on its back, and off they flew with Bean yelling to me that he'd meet me back at the flat.

Yeah, that's about the time the big UFO scare took place. We weren't being invaded by creatures from another planet, it was just an Unidentified Flying Dragon causing a blip on the airport radar.

That was the last I saw of Bean for the next three weeks. Then just as I was wondering if I should put his name in the Missing Persons column in the newspaper, he turned up to collect his stuff. Said he'd moved out to the desert. The dragon preferred it out there—the wide open spaces, plenty of heat, and feral pigs to feast on when he got hungry.

Bean gave me a forwarding address, just in case the producers of *Mad Max* were looking for extras, or anything like that.

Then he left, still owing me two weeks rent, the bastard.

I had to pay to get the whole flat fumigated to get rid of the smell on my own.

So this is the room. It could do with another coat of paint … unless you happen to be in to scorch marks as decoration? It's kind-of clean, and it's cheap. Are you going to take it or not?

By the way … don't have any pets, do you?

'No Pets Allowed' was accepted in 1986 by Pandora, *a glossy Australian gaming magazine, the sort that are widely distributed in newsagents and bookstores. It was to be my first professional sale and I was very excited. Then the magazine went out of print just before publication of the issue my story was to appear in. (Close, but no banana!) Showing the courage of his convictions, the editor, Merv Beamish, compiled the fiction and articles in a zine he paid to have printed called* Out of the Ashes. *You may have noticed that 'No Pets Allowed' was the first instalment of my* The Back of the Back of Beyond *universe, which was printed as a collection of interlinked short stories by Peggy Bright Books in 2013.*

Where the Last Humans Went

By midday another city looms in the distance, yet it stays elusive, out of our grasp. Night falls and my grandson and I pitch our tent, eat a meagre dinner and watch.

One light shines in one window in one apartment tower. No other signs of life there, but at least a glimmer of hope. So few people now.

My great-grandfather was a survivor of the generation who mostly pre-deceased their parents. Reckoned living on a farm with poor internet connection, doing daily physical work probably saved him. Still, he wouldn't have married Great-Grandma if he hadn't found her on the internet. Must have been love. She lived and worked with him on the farm with the poor internet connection the rest of her life.

Droughts and dust-storms brought Granddad knocking on the farmhouse door, begging for food. Grandma took a shine to him. They worked the land together, used the internet to trade their surplus crops and advertise for partners for their two children from an early age. But even though they got a few enquiries, no one wanted to leave the sanctuary of their own homes to travel, to meet, when they could interact on the internet.

I only met my own father a couple of times, mostly at funerals. Though he and Mum had a family of six kids in their internet world, in real life I was their only child.

I only had one child who only had one child; my grandson. No one of his age on the surrounding farms or in the surrounding towns. No transport left to take us long distances any more. Our electric car got stolen the first big city we stopped at. Never saw the thief, never saw signs of other people, though the internet and electricity were still available.

We kept journeying on foot.

There have been other cities. Mostly empty, except for animals and plants, reinhabiting what was originally theirs.

There must be other humans out there somewhere, still surviving somehow in concrete caves. Sometimes we touch them fleetingly through the web, but the merest suggestion that we meet face-to-face, rather than via electrons, has them scurrying away into silence.

So my grandson and I stalk lights in the darkness, trying to find him a mate. Surely the human race wasn't meant to end this way?

The next day we make the city. As dusk falls we see the light again, get our bearings, close in.

After a few questions, cautiously she opens the door. She is young—about my grandson's age—and she is beautiful. For a moment, old-fashioned hope flickers in my heart. Might she be interested in his company? Then I see the Aladdin's cave of technology piled behind her. She won't let us cross the threshold of her apartment, but she tells my grandson, with a shadow of a smile playing invitingly on her lips, that he can text her if he wants.

Published in Antipodean SF *issue 200, 2015. Editor: Ion Newcombe.*

A Harem of Six Legs

Little Master of Many Questions would have it that he stole me away from a desert camp, and we galloped along a valley between two lines of sand dunes, escaping into the night with only the moonlight to guide us. He would have it that the Caliph has put a price upon his head for stealing his favourite mare, and that he is a wanted man.

Man? With barely a wisp of a beard on his chin? And me a favoured mare? If only! I suspect the Caliph merely rolled his shoulders, no more irritated at losing me than if a gnat had bitten him when he was told that I was gone. He owns many horses, and I was nothing special—merely a flea-bitten grey mare with the kind eyes and dished face of my noble breed, lent out to visiting dignitaries to ride if their horses needed rest or had gone lame. And I was a breeding prospect.

I was due to be put to my Master's stallion, a mahogany bay, handsome enough, but a vain brute, given to biting, kicking and squealing to keep his harem in check. Known for killing his own male offspring before they were yearlings if they looked like they were going to be a challenge to him. Only really happy if he was showing off, or admiring his reflection in a pool of still water.

No thank you!

If Little Master of Many Questions hadn't chanced upon me, I would have nibbled through my tether rope and set myself free. His stealing me was a marriage of convenience.

He hadn't thought to steal a saddle or bridle when he stole me, so he was riding me bareback, in a light rope halter. As he reined me to a halt, I shifted my weight from hoof to hoof feeling his nervous tension flow through me.

"Which way? Which way?" he muttered to himself, looking about.

I should have known better but I said, "It all depends on where you want to go, young Master."

"To the palace of Zaziq," he replied.

I wondered how long it would be before he realized who he was talking to.

"You've spent the last hour heading in the opposite direction. You're going the wrong way." I spun around, pointing him in the direction he needed to go.

"Horse? You can talk?"

Oh, a quick learner! I liked him already.

"I can also read maps," I replied. "We want to go this way."

"Hmmm."

I swung my head around and saw his head tilted straight back. He was looking up at the night sky. Oh no! I didn't want to hear about following the Pole Star or how the left hand of the Water-Carrier pointed in the direction we had to go. I didn't want any arguments. I wasn't in the mood.

"Well, if you're sure..." he acquiesced.

A man who thought I could be right? He went up in my estimation. So we set out to get him where he wanted to go.

For a while he swayed on my back in silence. "My name's Tariq by the way," he introduced himself.

Might have been named for a star, but he didn't know how to read them! Not that I said that, of course.

"I'm Ahlam. Pleased to meet you. "

I could feel the question build in him before he said it. "Are you sure we're going the right way?"

"Yes, I'm sure. We might get there by dawn, unless you wanted to stop and sleep, of course."

"Not likely. I am now a horse thief. The Caliph's men are probably hunting us down."

"He's got plenty of horses. They probably haven't even noticed me missing, and if they have, the Horse Master will think I've come untethered and wandered off again."

As if I hadn't spoken, he went on. "They'll track us for many days, and at first we'll outrun them, but they'll corner us—perhaps at an oasis when we stop to drink. And I will put up a gallant fight and beat them all single-handed."

A story-teller as well as a thief. What were the odds?

"And I'll take all their gold and—"

"*What* gold? They're in the pay of the Caliph. He's so mean-hearted they'll be lucky to have coppers."

"And we'll refill our waterbags."

"These would be the waterbags you forgot to steal along with the saddle and bridle, would they?" I shouldn't have mentioned water, it reminded me that I was thirsty, and the nearest water was probably hours away.

"They'll have waterbags. We can take them."

"They'll have horses too. Fleeter of foot than me, no doubt. You could set me free and take one of them," I hinted.

"That wouldn't be right. We're friends now. Friends stick together."

I must be mad!

And I couldn't help myself, I had to ask, "Tell me, Little Master, will the Great and Mighty Zaziq be expecting you when we arrive? Will I be taken to his fabled stables where all the horses eat from silver dishes, and drink from marble fountains?" Did he think he was the only one with an imagination?

"Of course! And you will feast on pomegranates."

"I can't abide pomegranates," I told him, though I'd never tasted one.

"Dates then."

I considered this. It seemed acceptable. "And what will you eat, Little Master?"

"The Sultan will welcome me into his court, flattered by the gifts that I bring to him."

I nearly asked, "What gifts?" but I was getting the hang of this story-telling we were weaving between us as we went along.

"And he will hold a banquet to honour my arrival. We'll dine on roasted fowl and goat."

"Steady on, some of my friends are goats."

"Do they talk too?"

"Only the two-legged ones."

He laughed heartily at my joke. His voice dropped as he went on: "And for entertainment he will have several of his daughters dance for us."

No point informing him Sultans usually *don't* engage their own daughters as dancing girls, but keep them secreted away until they find a worthwhile suitor.

"And among them will be his fairest rose, his daughter Hiyam. And though her face is demurely veiled she will smile at me with her eyes."

"What if this Hiyam is ugly with buck-teeth and crossed eyes?" I asked, wondering what he was pinning his hopes on.

"Oh she's not! She's the most beautiful, wonderful … perfectly formed creature ever created," he sighed dreamily.

"You speak like you've met her."

"I have! But only in my dreams. I saw her at the marketplace once."

"You must be mistaken, Little Master. Sultans aren't renowned for letting their daughters walk freely among we common folk."

"She was accompanied by two enormous guards, and she had a companion with her."

Sounded plausible, I suppose, but not that common.

"Did she talk to you?"

"With her eyes," he said dreamily.

Oh boy! Did he have it bad!

Before I could ask, he continued, "They spoke to me of her captivity, of her longing to be free. I mean to grant her her freedom."

You mean to get yourself beheaded or worse, I thought, but wanting to be free—well, that was something I could relate to.

"And how will you set her free, Little Master? She will be locked behind palace walls, surely."

"Secretly, Ahlam, I am a Prince."

Secretly, I thought as I plodded along the trough between two sand dunes, *you are a dirty urchin with a vivid imagination.*

"And the Sultan will recognise that in you?" I queried my rider dressed in rags.

"Of course."

Of course not! What an innocent! A babe still wet behind the ears. The boy had *no idea* of what to do once he reached the Sultan's domain. He just expected all doors to be opened before him. Everyone would be bowing so low they wouldn't see he was wearing tattered rags, riding an Arabian mare he'd probably stolen from somewhere. Hmmm ... he was thinking how I'd expect a prince to think ...

"You don't believe me, Ahlam?"

The one thing I've learned about being a talking horse, it's not what you say, but what you don't say that counts.

"I didn't say that, Little Master. "

"But you thought it."

"Actually I was thinking we have a long way to go." And he was getting heavy, and I wished he'd offer to get off my back and walk beside me for a bit. But Little Master was getting tired. My four-footed gait was rocking him to sleep like a wet-nurse rocking a cradle. Every now and then his head would lull, and I'd feel the shock run through me as he jolted awake. Eventually he gave up the pretence, stretched his torso along my back and wrapped his arms around my neck. He was snoring before I had time to say, "Not on a first date!"

Without him awake to keep his balance, I had to try and keep it for him, shifting my weight subtly to counterbalance his supine form. Eventually he fell off, but I was up to my knees in sand by then, so he didn't have far to fall, and he had a soft landing.

He woke dazed and bewildered, blinking at me like a stupid owl in the moon-lit night. "Try walking for a bit," I suggested, and I didn't get the argument I expected. Instead he groped for the end of my tether to hold on to, and let me lead him through the desert.

After a few more hours of him stumbling behind me, he politely asked if I'd mind carrying him again. Well, I'd had some sort of rest, so I agreed. I actually made better progress that way. Every now and then he'd doze off, but he didn't fall off again.

"Wake up, Little Master!" I told him as dawn painted the land in pinks and golds. "Ahead lies the palace of the Sultan."

It was perched on a rock outcropping, adorned with minarets that looked like plump onions painted in swirls of peacock blue and gold. A ramshackle town had grown up below it, like children clustered around a mother's skirts.

"It's more beautiful than I remembered. Now what do we do?"

Excuse me? This was all his idea. I was just stolen goods.

"What were you planning we would do?" I asked, as he slid off my back and stood next to me, admiring the view.

"Sell the horse to get coins to buy some decent clothes."

"Now wait a minute!" I protested. That wasn't on my agenda at all. I was trying to get away from all this ownership nonsense, not get sold back into slavery.

"But that was before we became friends. And friends stick together."

I sighed in relief.

"But I don't know how I'll get decent clothes without any money."

"You're a thief, aren't you? How did you get me?"

"Oh!" The thought had never occurred to him. "And what about you?"

"Well, yes. If you could acquire some suitable livery for me, so I looked like a Prince's mount ..."

"But where would I find such things?"

Despite myself I rolled my eyes. Was it wise to be letting him chase after girls when clearly he still needed so much mothering? Did I have to do *everything* for him?

"Let's wander through the higgledy-piggledy town, Little Master. Surely they must have a saddle maker, and it's always washing day somewhere. Look casual though. Best not to draw attention to ourselves."

"A talking horse can do that."

I almost nipped him for his impudence.

He rode me down the back lanes to have a higher vantage point. I'd come to a stop behind the shop of a fabric weaver of dubious quality. I had seen a suitable piece of cloth for Little Master, and we were arguing.

"I'm not wearing that!" he protested in an angry whisper.

"It's the right length, and the colour will suffice at a pinch. It will make a good imitation of headdress and flowing robes, Tariq!"

"But it's a burial shroud, Ahlam—and a used one at that!"

Indeed it was—carefully washed to remove any evidence of its previous owner, and hanging on a washing line to dry, prior to being sold again to another unsuspecting buyer. I pitied the last occupant, lying stiff, dead and naked somewhere.

"Look, when opportunity presents itself, just grab it and run. At least that's my motto. Now take it, and we'll try to find something for me to wear."

He did as he was told, angrily rolling the shroud up and sitting awkwardly on it.

"We need to return to the main street now."

"But we'll be seen!" Tariq protested.

"That doesn't matter. I need to talk to any mules, donkeys or other horses that may be about."

"You can talk horse?" he asked me in all seriousness.

I turned my head to stare at him perched upon my back. What did he think he was riding?

He managed to look sheepish at my angry stare. He bobbed his head and even blushed becomingly. "Silly me. Of course you can," he apologised.

I strolled up to a small donkey overloaded with so many boxes and sacks I was surprised it could move at all.

I whinnied. It snorted, ears twitching in disbelief that a horse would speak respectfully to a donkey. They mostly all have inferiority complexes. I whinnied again and it brayed, giving me the information I needed. I neighed my thanks and wandered off, Little Master high on my back wondering what had just gone on.

"The blacksmith, just down the road here, has a merchant's horse in for new shoes," I told him. "Must be something special afoot (no pun intended) because it's rare to see a horse shod hereabouts. It just makes for extra weight to haul through the sand."

Speaking of hauling extra weight ...

"But I still don't understand ..." I really was beginning to wonder about him. He'd shown so much promise earlier on—at least some spark of intelligence.

"The horse was decked out in all its finery, which has been removed while its new shoes are fitted. In fact, I see them up ahead of us now."

The saddle had been set on a low branch of a tree. An elaborate bridle hanging off a branch beside it.

I walked up beside the saddle, telling Tariq, "Get that on me and be quick about it!"

He hopped off, swung the saddle up over my back and was just tightening the girth when the blacksmith spotted us. Tariq vaulted into the saddle, the bridle dangling off the crook of his arm. Unthinking, he kicked me in the sides a couple of times to spur me on, but I didn't need his encouragement, I was already galloping away as the blacksmith called uselessly after us: "Stop! Thief!"

I galloped straight out of town, pulling up only when I'd found a space between some rock outcroppings for us to hide, and for Tariq to change.

He approached my head to fit the bridle.

"I'm not wearing that bit, and that's final!" I decreed. It had sharp metal barbs in its centre, a device for torture.

"You're making me wear a used shroud," he countered.

"Your mouth's not likely to bleed from wearing a used shroud. Now unstrap that bit from the bridle," I stated firmly.

"But people will gawk at a man riding a horse with a bit-less bridle."

"They'll stare in awe that a man such as you can have such remarkable control over a beast like me with no restraining metal in my mouth. Now throw it away!"

He did so, and he grumbled again about wrapping a used shroud around himself too, but it did the trick. With part of the shroud twirled about his head like a loose turban, he fitted the role of a travel-weary nobleman. And I, dressed in borrowed finery, would hopefully be mistaken as a gentleman's mount.

Of course, I had no idea if this would work or not. If either one of us slipped out of character, then the game was lost …well, alright, if *he* slipped out of character. If *I* slipped out of character, I'd still be a horse.

Head held high, I pranced up to the guards at the outer gate to the Sultan's palace, hoping Little Master would remember what to say.

In the end he didn't have to. The guards raised their hands in welcome, calling "Abdul, the merchant! The Sultan is waiting to see you."

Now there was a stroke of luck! I only wondered what Tariq would produce as samples of his wares, or what excuse he'd use to get to see Hiyam. Oh well, it wasn't my problem. I couldn't be expected to do everything, could I?

We were shown through to an inner courtyard. Tariq dismounted, but I wasn't led off to the stables as I'd expected. A tall, thin man with an elaborate headdress and grey robes came forth to greet Tariq.

"But merchant, where are your goods?" he asked, not seeing any samples of wares.

Little Master dug through the folds of the shroud. In truth, I thought he was scratching at a flea bite, but from somewhere he brought forth a small pouch, which he opened, pouring the contents onto his palm. My ears pricked with interest. Gemstones, diamonds. I wondered where he'd stolen those from.

It was enough to catch the other man's attention.

"I hear the Sultan has many beautiful daughters? I hope these gems might interest them."

Oh, my clever boy! What woman can resist jewels?

I felt apprehensive as Tariq was led into the inner sanctum of the Sultan's domain and I lost sight of him. Nervously I shifted my weight from one hoof to another. Would he get to see his Hiyam? Would he say something stupid and give the game away? I was also alert for horses' hooves thundering up the path to the Sultan's outer gates. How much time did we have before the real merchant came to the Sultan complaining he'd been robbed? Or even the shroud seller for that matter.

"Ahlam! Come quick, Ahlam!" Little Master's voice called urgently for me from somewhere in the palace. I didn't think twice, but set off at a gallop into the grand building to try and find him.

I found him surrounded by girls—the Sultan's daughters and perhaps a few of his younger wives. He was smiling broadly, and I was puzzled. He gave a slight nod meant only for me, and said to his attentive female audience. "You see how obedient my beautiful horse is?"

"But is she fast?" one girl asked.

"You saw how fast she found me, didn't you? And she's so gentle with it. Come and stroke her velvet nose."

I couldn't believe it! We were both risking life and death and he was busy flirting!

A small dainty hand reached out to stroke my muzzle. I looked into her eyes and saw a longing for freedom there, and at once knew who this girl was. Oh clever Little Master! Oh clever young girl!

"Would you like to ride her? Just sit on her back to see how kind my mare is?" Tariq suggested.

"Yes, I would." She signalled to a eunuch nearby (a Sultan's daughter was not to be touched by strangers!) and he lifted her onto my back. It was like being ridden by a feather! But next Little Master was swinging himself up onto my back behind the girl.

He threw the pouch of gems behind him, explaining, "Here is your sister's dowry!" before he spurred me on, crying, "Run like the wind, Ahlam!" which I did.

The outer gates to the Sultan's palace were open, the guards in conversation with the real merchant who'd arrived bareback on his horse.

"That's the culprit! Stop Thief!" he cried as we sped past him, quite upsetting his horse which made a diversion of its own.

I didn't quite hear the rest of the words that were shouted after us, I was too busy escaping.

I headed back to the rock outcropping where we'd both changed before, and came to a halt.

"Best to leave the merchant's saddle and bridle where it can be found, don't you think?" I asked Tariq.

Posing to impress his girl, he said nonchalantly, "I'm already a horse thief. How much worse can it get?"

"Well, if you want the saddle, *you* can wear it. I'm not going to!" I stated, noting he was already unwinding himself from the 'princely robes' of his borrowed shroud.

"Alright, I get your point! As long as I can leave this shroud as well."

"And when are you intending to formally introduce me to Hiyam?" I asked.

He rolled his eyes at me then. "We're being chased and you're resting on formalities! Hiyam, I'd like to introduce you to my spectacular friend, the horse, Ahlam. Ahlam, this is Hiyam, whose image has burned in my heart since the day I first set eyes on her."

"Your horse talks?" Wasn't it obvious? And why did they *all* say that? But then the dear thing redeemed herself in my eyes by turning to me, bowing her head and saying "I'm honoured to meet you, Ahlam. Thank you for saving me."

"My pleasure, my dear—but I don't think we're quite safe yet. Let's make haste now."

"Perhaps Hiyam would prefer to ride in a saddle?" Tariq pondered.

"I'm quite comfortable riding bareback, thank you. I've ridden horses all my life."

Ooh, I liked her already. She had an air of independence and feistiness about her, as well as gentleness and kindness.

Tariq fumbled awkwardly around her, wanting to help her onto my back, but at the same time respect her dignity by not touching her. I don't know who was the more surprised as she sprung nimbly onto my back without his assistance.

We left the saddle, bridle and shroud on the road into the town, then we set off in the opposite direction. I was determined to put as much distance between us and the Sultan's palace as possible.

"So you're a human thief now as well as a horse thief, Little Master?" I asked him when we finally stopped for a rest.

"You saw me leave that bag of gems for Hiyam's dowry," Tariq told me indignantly.

Which he got from where, exactly? I'd probably have to sort that one out as well. "Where to now?" I asked.

"My father's palace, I think. For I really am a Prince, as I told you."

And I'm the Queen of Sheba's White Ass! I thought, but I said, "Hiyam, you'll get used to his tall stories."

"No, Ahlam, truly I am a Prince. Can you find your way to the Northern Road? We need to travel on it for three days until we reach my father's palace, but right now I need to get acquainted with my beautiful Hiyam."

"Of course, Little Master."

And what do you know? Three days later, I found myself standing in front of another palace, where my rag-tag waif of a horse-stealing friend was welcomed as a long lost son! The Sultan's daughter was also welcomed, and his flea-bitten grey Arabian mare was led to the most opulent stables she's ever seen in her life! I am offered the sweetest water to drink from an alabaster bowl (marble is *so* overstated, don't you think?) and the freshest, cleanest hay. And even dates when I have a fancy for them. But no pomegranates!

And I accept all this as if it's my due, for Little Master of Many Questions and I are friends ... and friends look out for each other.

'A Harem With Six Legs' is published for the first time in this collection.

Teach Your Children Well

"Remember the rabbit," my sister hissed to me as we stood before the pale, prone body of my father on the hospital bed, connected to machines that kept him alive while they sucked away our meagre inheritance by the hour.

He'd been out to it for five days now. The hospital staff had seen my sister and me pale by degrees as they'd talked about the latest treatments. Nanos would keep him stable until replacement organs could be generated from tissue samples, then inserted. All for a cost, of course.

Everyone we spoke to from the hospital seemed caring on the outside, but with hard-rock eyes that said "You really can't afford this, can you?" when we responded with stunned mullet shock instead of eagerly agreeing to all the procedures they suggested, no matter the cost. They started dropping hints about needing their bed back, suggested organ harvesting to help pay the bills already accumulated. Dad wasn't really old, and had been in good health until …

I wanted to consider it, but the only support my sister gave me was, "Remember the rabbit!"

How old had we been when we'd pleaded with our parents to get us a rabbit? Swearing we'd both care for it, promising to feed it, groom it, clean its hutch.

Fur as soft as silk, twitching nose, we took turns to have it nestled in our arms, fought over who would brush it, who would feed it, who would clean its hutch ... at least for the first three weeks. But the novelty soon wore off. We were children after all, and easily distracted. Parents gave up bullying us into feeding and hutch-cleaning duties and took on the responsibilities themselves as we were caught up with the latest interest. When we finally recalled we had a rabbit and plucked it out of the hutch to play with again, it had scratched us. We didn't want it any more.

Dad hadn't prettied it up with illusions of sending Flopsie to a farm or anything. If we didn't want the rabbit anymore, it went on a one-way trip to the vet. He didn't let us off the hook with that either. We had to stay and bear witness to Flopsie's final moments, watch its nose stop twitching and bunny eyes stare blank and lifeless as the life seeped out of it. Its soul hopefully escaped to rabbit heaven.

Flopsie conveniently disposed of, we could get on with our lives. I never told anyone but I had nightmares for months after, though I finally outgrew them—or thought I did, until today when it all came flooding back.

How long had it been since we'd done anything with Dad? Acted like a family? Not since before Mum had died. My sister and I had left home, gone on to make our own lives. Like the rabbit, Dad was redundant now. In silent agreement, we sought a hard-eyed doctor to tell our decision to.

Published in Antipodean SF *issue 164 (2012). Editor: Ion Newcombe.*

Only Women Bleed

The young woman's face, in death, seemed to have an almost incandescent beauty. Her head was turned to her left and she had a certain calm, as if she were merely watching someone leave the deserted wharf warehouse where her body had been found by a security guard doing his midnight rounds.

Chief Inspector Harris wondered how a woman so young could be murdered so brutally and yet still look so at peace. He crouched low, close to her head, as if by doing so she could whisper the name of her murderer in his ear from the great beyond.

As best he could, he tried to follow her line of sight. It provided no clue. She merely looked towards a far corner of the warehouse where a sheet of roofing iron had torn loose, forming a hole. No doubt it was big enough for a man to fit through, but the warehouse roof was easily three stories high. A man would risk breaking his neck if breaking in, and would need a cherry picker or a fireman's ladder if breaking out. Harris glanced around the warehouse to make sure such things weren't nearby.

Nor was the murderer's image trapped in the girl's blue eyes.

She was expensively attired, if he wasn't mistaken, and he rarely was. Her short red sequined dress hung in shreds intermingled with her torn flesh and blood.

Harris suspected that a knife had been used in a frenzied attack to cause such damage, but if that was the murder weapon, it had been conveniently misplaced.

There was something odd about the corpse that Harris couldn't quite work out. A ruby ring sat on her blood-splattered right hand, a silent testimony that robbery hadn't been the motive for such a grisly death.

He shivered in the pre-dawn cool. It was summer: the day would warm up soon enough. Best to have the young lady resting on a cool slab in the morgue by then.

"She got anything to say?"

Harris straightened, startled by the voice behind him. It belonged to Smithy from Forensics, who had the black sense of humour you needed to survive his line of work, mostly dealing with corpses day in and day out. Smithy's hair was a shock of pure white. He was closer to retirement than Harris, having got into the game in the days before 'forensic' had 'science' attached to it. To his credit, technology and learning had never daunted him. He could handle a computer with the best of them.

Smithy peered over Harris's shoulder. "Christ! I've got a daughter at home no older than her. What a mess!"

"Knife attack?" Harris conjectured, rising to his feet and taking a step back from the corpse to allow Smithy a better view.

"Maybe."

There was a snap of latex as Smithy donned his surgical gloves. He was already wearing his white disposable cover-all. That combined with his white hair made him look more ghostly than the corpse did. He bent to have a closer look at the wounds.

"She looks like she's been gutted, ripped from crux to sternum."

Harris swallowed, never keen on Smithy's florid descriptions. "I'll read it in your report, Mat."

"It was pretty bloody frenzied, whatever it was," Smithy went on in his 'off-the-cuff' style.

"Bloody being the operative word," Harris commented dryly.

"Actually, no. That's the odd thing about it, there isn't a lot of blood around at all. Come have a closer look."

Harris regarded the body again. He'd seen enough murder victims in his time to know better, he should have picked up on that. Maybe the red of her dress had distracted him? Or maybe he was getting too old for this game?

The security guard who'd made the gruesome discovery and the two constables who had responded to the initial call all kept a safe distance and did their best not to look at the young woman's body. The younger of the two constables was looking decidedly pale, the other seemed to be holding up alright, and the security guard just looked weary. It had been a long night for him, and would no doubt grow longer before he was able to go home, but he seemed resigned to his lot, as if he'd encountered this sort of thing before and knew the drill. Nothing about him suggested that he was anything other than an unfortunate bystander who had found the body, but Harris would have to question him and the constables anyway.

A couple of other white-attired forensic people were entering the warehouse. It was still eerily quiet as Harris backed away from the corpse and left Smithy and his helpers to get on with solving their piece of the puzzle.

Annabella was a small but stately lady in her middle years. Her poise and dress whispered of wealth. She had an air of tranquillity which came from knowing that if she had a need in life, she had the resources to buy it. Not a bad state of affairs for someone whose job description fell between loyal servant and mistress.

But now she was reaching the end of her usefulness. It was time to consider an early retirement from her employer and appoint her successor. She had placed advertisements around the local university and had been deluged with applications from young women. Though many of the applicants were suitable, Annabella had finally selected Eve.

Eve studied Arts. She was vivacious, pretty and broad-minded. She also had a bubbly sense of humour—a facet which Annabella lacked, more so now that she was coming to the end of her womanhood. Annabella faced the Change with a certain bitterness. She envied Eve her youth, wishing that she could have her years all over again to go on serving the Master.

When Annabella had explained the … darker … side of the job, Eve's eyes had gone wide, but she'd licked her lips in anticipation. She would have no qualms about that part of her work.

Now they sat in awkward silence in Annabella's apartment, waiting to be driven to dinner at the Master's.

"His car should be here presently. Is there anything else you wish to ask me about the position?" Annabella inquired finally.

Eve merely shook her head as her eyes scanned the sitting room, taking in the expensive array of antiques and curios scattered on the fine furniture. All were gifts or 'hand-me-downs' given to Annabella by the Master for her loyalty and service.

A buzz from the intercom signalled that the Master's chauffeur had arrived and was waiting for them downstairs. They left the carpark of the building as the last light of sunset was fading from the sky.

Despite Annabella living within walking distance of her employer's residence, he had insisted on sending the car to collect her and Eve. As the women made themselves comfortable in the car's back seat, Annabella realised the logic behind his move:

it gave her another chance to assess Eve. Though obviously in awe of the wealth that was purposefully being displayed to her, Eve maintained her poise and grace, managing to act as if she were accustomed to such a life. It was one more test that she had unwittingly passed with flying colours.

Like the rest of the house, the Master's dining room was opulently furnished. He had a penchant for dark wood: table, chairs, sideboard and so on, all polished to a low sheen to suggest warmth in the room. The lighting was low. Candles set in golden candelabra supplied a soft light as the dinner party ate off fine china using gold-plated cutlery that gently reflected the candlelight. They drank their water and wine from antique crystal in honour of their special guest.

Annabella continued her observations all through dinner and found Eve's manners well above standard. The girl didn't over-indulge in the wine she was offered (another good sign) and though she'd been demure when in Annabella's apartment, her vibrant personality came to the fore at the dinner table. She was engaging to talk to, and she could make the Master laugh. Annabella could tell by the half-smile that stayed on the Master's lips all throughout dinner that he was enchanted with Annabella's protégé. Occasionally he would look directly at Annabella, conveying a silent message: *You have served me well.*

Annabella would lower her lashes in response, partly because she was still shy of his flattery even after all these years, partly because she didn't want him witnessing the distress surrendering her vocation to a younger woman was causing her.

There was more than loyalty in Annabella's service to him. She loved her employer, Tregear, with all her heart. He was pleasing to the eye with his youthful face, piercing blue eyes, shoulder-length waved copper hair and his elegantly trimmed goatee. His passion was people, and his strong personality drew people to him like moths to a flame. He loved to entertain and be entertained and all were equal in his eyes, friends and servants alike; and he liked showering them with extravagant gifts, as if to pay penance for his enormous wealth.

If Eve could serve him loyally, maybe even fall in love with Tregear the way Annabella had, then the girl would lead a happy and contended life before handing her position on to somebody else. Yet it hurt Annabella to let the man go after all their years together. She had been his first, after all.

After brandy and chocolates, the conversation was flagging and the night was moving on.

"Annabella has explained my little passion to you, my dear?" Tregear inquired.

"Yes, she has," Eve replied, with a little catch of anticipation in her voice.

"And you're at that special time of the month?"

"Yes, I am," Eve said, looking demurely at the table.

"And a virgin as well?" Tregear pushed to know her intimately, even though Annabella had already been very thorough and precise with her questioning.

"Yes." Eve's voice was barely a whisper. She blushed, making her more beautiful to Tregear.

"Then I think we will retire now."

Tregear rose, cupped Annabella's face gently in his hands and kissed her lightly on her lips. "Charles will see you home," he said to her. "I'll contact you tomorrow evening."

Tregear turned and took Eve by her arm, escorting her through the darkened halls towards his bedroom. He didn't spare a backward glance for Annabella, though he knew she continued to watch him.

Like the dining room, Tregear's bedroom was furnished in dark polished wood. The bed was king-sized and inviting, the bedhead made of ornately carved wooden rungs. An anglaise bedspread hinted at a woman's touch. Once again, the lighting was subdued, though from a bedside lamp rather than candlelight.

Eve took in these details through a cursory glance around the room as she entered, before Tregear gently turned her to face him. He took exquisite care in undressing Eve, content to take his time.

Briefed by Annabella, Eve kept silent. The wine she had consumed through dinner, and the brandy after, helped soothe her; and Tregear's very presence seemed almost hypnotically relaxing. When he'd fully disrobed her, she stood before him as beautiful and pale as any statue.

"There's no need to be afraid," Tregear told her quietly as he stroked her short hair, letting his fingers capture the wisps of her curls.

"I'm not," Eve replied, composed if not confident.

He tipped her chin up so that he could taste her lips. She warmed to him at once, her arms wrapping around his neck as their tongues duelled. His hands skimmed lightly over her. She pressed the length of her body against him, hungry for more.

Gracefully, Tregear lifted her into his arms and carried her the few steps to the bed where she stretched out, her lips still hot on his. He settled himself over her, then began to kiss at her jawline. Eve moaned softly, the sound exquisite as she offered her neck to him. He kissed her there, almost intoxicated by the racing throb as his lips embraced her pulse point. He knew better than to linger, greater joys awaited him further down her body. Her breasts were particularly sensitive. With tongue and teeth alone playing on her nipples, he brought her to climax as she clung to the rungs of the bedhead and gasped. Tregear rested his head between her pale breasts momentarily, giving her time to recover. The closeness of her beating heart thrilled him and soon he had to push himself away, his kisses spiralling down her body until he nuzzled her clitoris. That small attention had Eve writhing with pleasure again. His tongue unfolded her, feathered its way down to her most delightful cavern.

By now he could smell her blood, it added to his excitement, his erection straining against the material of his finely tailored trousers. He entered her with his tongue, the rich taste of her blood sending shivers running through him. Eve cried out, wrapping her legs around him in her eagerness, drawing him closer to her like a bug trapped in a spider's web. Tregear loved that best, being shrouded by her flesh as she writhed around him and he feasted on her offerings.

Eve arched and moaned, coming again and again until her grip on him relaxed and, spent, she whimpered, falling into an exhausted sleep.

Tregear smiled to himself, satisfied that he still had the artfulness to render a woman unconscious so pleasurably. Regretfully, he left her, but before he did he lightly covered her with a blanket and kissed her on the forehead, fatherly fashion. She would sleep, content, no doubt, but with his energy renewed, he was keen to explore the night.

When he next caught up with Annabella, he would present her with some small token of his affection, because he couldn't supress the feeling that he was betraying her loyalty despite them both knowing the truth.

While she could, Annabella still offered herself to him, but her cycles were becoming further apart, like a dying planet in an erratic orbit. He wished he had some way to alter the course her life was taking. He knew how much she'd loved him, loved him still, been tolerant of his little indulgences with other women. They were always used for sexual release, while it had always been Annabella who'd fed him. Only Annabella had shared his secrets … until now.

Though Annabella had kept her good looks, she was no longer young. And despite the many gifts Tregear lavished on her, youthfulness and immortality were two gifts he could not bestow. He could not deny the fact that she would continue to grow old and would eventually die. That thought always returned to haunt him.

Eve began accompanying Tregear on social outings. He paid her a generous allowance that was comparable to a good salary. Cash in hand, no records kept. Like a china doll, he dressed her up in glorious creations she could never afford, so that she looked pretty when she went out with him. There was also an upgrade in her make-up, and lessons on how to apply it for best effect.

Yet he never showed an interest in bedding her unless she was in blood. Then it would be a glorious week of orgasm after orgasm that left them both sated—him for another month apparently. For the rest of the time she was always dropped off safely at her apartment at the end of the evening and kissed chastely on the lips.

Eve wondered if he then went off to sleep with Annabella, who had accompanied them on their first few outings until Eve had stated, in a way that was only half-humorous, that she didn't need a chaperone. Annabella had begged off some invitations after that. But the crone still seemed to have a powerful hold over Tregear.

Tregear had two distinct circles of friends. He knew the Goths, those dark-lidded, dark-lipped, dark-dressed lost young things who haunted shadowy places. Their talk was of death and darkness. They seemed drawn to Tregear, despite his being older than most of them.

For them he dressed in velvet frock coats and elaborate linen shirts with ruffles at neck and wrists. He dressed in colours of claret, emerald or midnight blue, and shone like a jewel when he sat among them, holding court about ancient graveyards, long dead poets and archaeology.

Eve tried to stay attentive at such events, but it wasn't always easy. This wasn't her crowd at all and she never really felt comfortable in their presence.

The gathering points of the rich and famous were his other favourite social arena. There he was an understated jewel, but a jewel nonetheless; dressing more to blend in than to stand out.

The conversations tended more towards the political, the stock-market and the latest social trends. Here Tregear was one amongst many voices, when he chose to speak, although sometimes his evenings out amongst this crowd seemed more to do with silent contemplation.

Eve kept her ears and eyes open at such occasions, being seen, getting known, smiling with this one, chatting with that one; who knew where a little subtle networking could lead? She was constantly bemused at how Tregear could be perfectly and effortlessly at ease in two such diverse worlds, yet he was.

No matter what group he was with, they accepted Eve not for who she was, but because she was with Tregear. She enjoyed the power of being associated with him.

The barrier between employer and servant was fast being eroded, they were becoming friends. Yet Tregear's love for Annabella was a hard spell to break. Eve had quickly worked out that there was a deep and abiding love between those two, and Annabella always seemed to be hovering in the background, on the periphery of his subconscious, always just a split-second away in Tregear's thoughts. Eve knew that she could never be as selflessly devoted to Tregear as Annabella had been and still was. She wasn't about to fall in love with the boss. He was a good person to work for and work with; they shared laughter and good times. And though peculiar, she couldn't say it was a demanding job, but she was determined to have a life of her own when Tregear didn't need her; all the more so when she suspected he was having normal sex with other women.

"All the Goths call you a vampire," Eve said with what she hoped was the right amount of cheerful jokiness. Tregear had just made love to her in his usual fashion, she was feeling relaxed and content and this was her effort at pillow-talk.

With cheeks flushed from exertion and renewed vigour, Tregear rolled on his back next to her on his big bed and laughed. "And you've suspected they're right for months now, I know."

He had that half-smile on his lips that Eve recognised from the verbal jousting-matches he sometimes got into with some of the Goths when they pressed him on what he was.

He loved to play cat-and-mouse with them, stringing them along with noncommittal answers, teasing and frustrating them. She suspected he would lead her the same merry dance. He stayed silent, the next move was hers.

"But I've seen you eat garlic," Eve stated.

Tregear's smile widened. He nodded, waiting for her to draw other comparisons.

"And wear crosses."

"You'll remember how we sheltered from the storm in a church foyer that night," Tregear said, providing her with another contradiction to confound her. (He'd foolishly told his driver they'd be walking home.) "And you've seen me preening myself in front of mirrors often enough." He was a veritable peacock, always flattered by his own reflection.

"Alright, so it's silly to believe in vampires, and you're not one?"

"On the contrary, my dear, I am one. I've had the blood fever ever since my Maker mingled our blood."

Unconscious of her actions, she skittered away from him a little on the bed.

"But you haven't killed me." Eve realised she'd said what was on her mind before fully thinking it through, wondered if he was about to confess to killing a score of other girls before telling her she'd be next.

"Nor do I intend to," Tregear reassured her. "We are not the power-hungry, blood-starved creatures portrayed in fiction, you know. We aren't driven out into the streets each night in search of sacrificial victims. If we did that, we'd end up killed, locked up in prisons, or sent away to mad-houses." He seemed to dwell on that last prospect as if it meant something personal to him. "We choose more subtle ways in these ... politically correct times.

You give your blood freely to me each month and that combined with an occasional blue steak gets me by. Though I do have a supply of cows' blood on hand if I find my strength ebbing."

"Could you just survive drinking animal blood?"

He considered his answer. It had been said that the need for human blood was merely a psychological offshoot of the disease, or possibly the myth that had travelled down through history with it, but it was a craving that he had never dared try to ignore. He remembered the blood-lust all too well, causing his brief but violent madness in the past.

"Possibly," he conceded. "Though I think chasing rats is most undignified and I'm yet to find a supermarket selling delicacies to people … of my persuasion." Again he laughed. Vampire movies made him uncomfortable, but he'd seen his share, if only to keep up with the fashions of pop culture.

"Yet you've always refused to drink blood at the Goth hangouts," Eve said, remembering how it seemed to be a show of bravado with those dark children.

Tregear reacted with horrified distaste, "Of course I have! Most of those beverages are laced with drugs of some sort, and who knows what diseases you might catch from drinking that blood! We're not immortal, you know."

Another urban myth shattered. But it explained why Eve had to have a blood test before she was given this position. He knew she was clean and pure.

"So how old are you then?" Eve asked.

Tregear answered with a question of his own, "How old do you think I am?" His eyebrow arched up as he inquired, instantly putting her on her guard.

Knowing his fastidiousness over his appearance, Eve chose her answer carefully. "Somewhere in your late thirties?"

"What?" came the outraged response. Tregear pulled at his cheeks, peering at his reflection in the dressing table mirror. "I thought I was passing myself off as someone in their late twenties! Would I look younger if I shaved off the beard?" He stroked his goatee distractedly. "Though not too bad for someone who's in his late seventies, I suppose."

"Never!" Eve exclaimed her disbelief, not sure if he was playing games with her. Yet he responded seriously.

"The diet certainly helps with the longevity, or perhaps the disease does. I can expect to live another fifty or sixty years, perhaps longer if I'm careful, and nobody blows the planet up first." For a moment his mind wandered and he thought of how many of those years would be without Annabella; or Eve for that matter.

Eve's mouth became a perfect 'O' of amazement, which pulled him away from his morbid thoughts. The look on her face made him laugh. "Surprised? You'll find through your association with me you'll postpone the ravages of age for a time. Annabella certainly has. It's a fringe-benefit of the job that no one's been able to explain. Now, catch up on your beauty sleep, I've an appointment to keep." Tregear kissed Eve on the forehead father-fashion and rose to get changed.

He was half-way to his walk-in wardrobe when Eve's statement reached him: "You're going to see Annabella, aren't you?"

Tregear came to a halt, didn't bother to turn and face her as he asked, "What of it?" His voice was spiked with warning.

Knowing she had reached a point it would be unwise to cross, Eve backed down. "Oh, nothing. Have a nice time."

Tregear heard a rustle as Eve settled herself in his bed. She was feigning sleep when he departed and would be gone by the time he returned.

*

"The little one has worked out my secret at last," Tregear reported to Annabella a short time later when they met up in a late-night café for coffee and to talk.

She knew that playful look he gave her; he loved his little intrigues. An inquiring mind had been an essential prerequisite in selecting her replacement. Annabella thought back to her own initiation, all those years ago, into the sinister world that Tregear had inhabited. A product of her time, Annabella had been more alarmed by his unusual, though delightful, sexual practices than she'd been by his declaration that he needed her blood to survive.

"You seem happy with her," she noted.

"She is a delight!" Tregear admitted. Quickly he looked into Annabella's eyes, as if catching himself on the verge of making a gross mistake. "But she's not you. She'll never truly replace you, Annabella."

Annabella offered a tight-lipped smile and reached across the small table where they sat to squeeze his hand. She tried to be philosophical. "The world is changing."

"I always loved you, though I might not have always shown it."

She said nothing, but the look in her eyes reassured him that his feelings were reciprocated and always had been. He'd been the centre of her life for so many years and still was; she'd do anything—say anything—to protect him, which was why she said now, "In time, Tregear, I'm sure you'll come to feel more strongly about Eve."

"Perhaps."

To the observer they merely seemed a handsome young man with a fixation on an older woman. It amused Annabella momentarily, but could not obscure the pain. Soon she'd be of little practical use to Tregear. She'd been very brave about it all, but she just could not give Tregear up entirely. Neither, it now seemed, could he sever his ties with her.

Seeing the sorrow written on her face, Tregear asked, "What could I give you to make you happy?"

"I wish I could be young again," Annabella answered wistfully. Silently she added, *I wish I could be like you.*

Unlike Annabella, who had always focused all her attention on Tregear, Eve seemed distracted whenever they went out. Her mind was not totally on him, which did nothing for his ego.

Now she looked preoccupied as she sat at his dining room table, unaware of the frown that creased her brow as she waited to accompany him to a theatre premier.

"You look worried, my dear. Is everything all right?" Tregear asked his distracted beauty.

Eve shrugged. "My studies, I guess."

Tregear felt there was something that she was hiding from him. Unlike Annabella, Eve rarely shared her secrets with him, and he missed those intimacies, feeling that he was inextricably connected to another's life. Eve saw her engagement as his companion as a pleasant part-time job, but not a vocation. It had been wrong to think that someone else could mould themselves effortlessly into the role Annabella had occupied for so long.

Despite his misgivings about Eve, Tregear felt uplifted by the first hints of spring in the air. The social set was beginning to stir and stretch its wings; invitations were once again coming in thick and fast.

"I trust you'll accompany me to the Harding's Ball next Saturday evening?" Tregear inquired of Eve, hoping to raise her spirits; she'd seemed a little down of late. Eve merely nodded, not even making eye contact with him; not the response he'd expected.

With a magician's flourish, Tregear produced ten crisp hundred-dollar notes which he presented to Eve arrayed as a fan. "Why don't you go and buy yourself something nice?"

Eve took the proffered money and forced herself to smile. "Thank you, Tregear."

Always cash. Though old-fashioned, it was untraceable. More than once she'd bent the truth, told him something had cost more than it had to buy and pocketed the difference. The money he'd just given her was enough to buy her way out of her present troubles. She could wear one of the other dresses that she'd bought with his money, he'd barely notice. Or she could just disappear, send him her resignation by text message. How had she allowed her life to become so complicated? She should never had become involved with Tregear and the people he knew.

"A nice little cocktail dress, perhaps," Tregear's voice interrupted her private thoughts. "And aren't you a little late this month?"

"Stress," Eve replied, hoping that was all it was. She had discreetly taken a lover, a young man plucked from Tregear's affluent friends, a real lover who could fill her with more than just his tongue. Obviously, because of her services to Tregear, she couldn't go on the pill, but they'd been taking precautions. If she was pregnant, it would mean the end of her blood money, but he could find someone else to fulfil his needs; he'd found her easily enough.

Unwilling to confront the possibility of being pregnant, Eve took Tregear's money and bought herself a skimpy little red sequined party dress. She'd told her boyfriend, Philip, about how Tregear liked to think he was a vampire (keeping the other details to herself). Full of lust and bravado, Philip had told her she should allow the rich their little eccentricities. There was no such thing as vampires, but if, by chance, there were, he'd protect her from them. She'd felt safe in his arms, and foolish for believing Tregear.

*

Annabella was being a wall-flower at the Ball. Beautifully dressed, she tried to mingle with the older crowd who all knew her and were alternately scandalised and sympathetic that she was no longer escorted by Tregear. As the Ball revolved around her, her eyes kept straying to Tregear who looked pale and showed none of his usual exuberance.

While he explained to others that he was recovering from a dose of the 'flu, Annabella knew what really ailed him. Her worried eyes followed his movements, while Eve—her dress the colour of the blood Tregear craved—flittered about, enjoying the limelight, unaware of the anguish she was causing Tregear by not giving him what he wanted.

It wasn't right, Annabella thought, this depending on just one woman to fulfil his needs. It had been different when she was serving Tregear, because her unshakeable love for him had meant that she was completely loyal. She should have hired two women, or maybe more, to take over her role. Maybe she should go hunting for another young student to bring in to their exclusive little club.

As if aware of Annabella's scrutiny, Eve glared at her across the crowded hall. Her look was a challenge, as if she knew she had the one thing that Annabella most wanted.

Annabella scowled back, jealous of Eve's place by Tregear's side.

Whenever they met at social functions they circled each other like a couple of wary cats, neither of them sure of their standing.

Tregear spent the night palming Eve off to one male after another. She had made an impression with those he knew, and had many admirers. She was as keen to dance with them as Tregear was to have her away from his immediate company tonight, though usually he preferred to keep her close by.

With Eve safely ensconced on the dance floor, Annabella approached Tregear, who sat on a chair looking pale and weary. She kissed him lightly on the cheek in greeting and sat down beside him, intent on telling him he should arrange for at least another woman to cater to his needs.

"She hasn't been feeding you, has she?" Annabella inquired euphemistically.

"It's the stress of her studies making her a little late," Tregear apologised on Eve's behalf.

"Not a little pregnant?" Annabella hissed.

Tregear paled even more when confronted with this possibility. He'd considered it, of course, but had presumed that Eve would stay loyal to him the way Annabella had.

"I was in the ladies' powder room—I overheard a relevant piece of gossip ..." Annabella purposefully let her sentence hang.

Tregear slumped, then turned his pained eyes to Annabella. "How could she betray me?"

Self-satisfied, Annabella watched as disappointment gave way to anger in Tregear; it was an emotion he had not permitted himself to experience in many years. The anger ignited his blood-lust and he knew he had to get out of this public place.

There was no courtesy shown to the man Eve danced with. He was young, well-connected, and in a glance Tregear surmised that he was very likely the father of Eve's child. Tregear grabbed Eve by the wrist territorially.

"I'm not feeling well." Tregear's words were sharp, cold, like shards of ice. "It's best we leave."

"But Tregear—" Eve tried to protest.

"I insist. I brought you here, I should escort you home."

He nearly pulled her off her feet as he dragged her from the now silent dance floor. Eve glanced back over her shoulder to

Philip, confusion clear on her face. Was it possible that Tregear had found out about her affair?

A sea of puzzled faces stared back at her. This drama would give them something to gossip about for weeks. The way he took possession of her and dragged her off like that; so dramatic, so theatrical, so Tregear!

Eve was vaguely aware that somewhere behind her, beyond the people who gasped and stared, Annabella was standing with her back to a wall, and she was smiling.

Perhaps it was shock, or the almost hypnotic control that Tregear seemed to have over her now that deadened Eve's senses as he propelled her through the deserted late-night streets. She knew she was in trouble, that she should try to escape, but she could not. Like a rabbit mesmerised by the headlights of the on-coming car, some part of Eve was compelled to watch this drama unfold, even though she already knew how it would end.

They were down amongst the piers and the warehouses that still made up the working part of the harbour, surrounded by silence and long shadows. Tregear kept a tight hold of the girl's arm, kept propelling her forward, marching her along the shortest route he knew to his house, making for the sanctuary of home.

But he wasn't going to make it. The distance was just too far, and the blood-lust that he'd kept under control for years was now too great upon Tregear, compelling him to feed.

A short way ahead he saw a single security guard emerge from a side-door of a warehouse, noted that he'd left it unlocked, but had continued on and showed no signs of coming back. Tregear changed his direction, pushed Eve through the unlocked door and into the vast expanse beyond.

Enraged, Tregear accused her of being unfaithful to him.

"Being your escort is only a job," Eve reminded him in a distant, trembling voice.

Job? *Job!* He'd offered her so much more than that, and he knew it. "And part of your *job*"—he all but spat the word in her face—"was to stay faithful to *me*! To give yourself to no other. Certainly not to become *pregnant* and make yourself useless to my needs!"

She was silent when he accused her of being pregnant, but her hand moved to rest protectively across her abdomen as she wondered where her real lover was. Surely Philip must have followed them from the ball?

Her subtle movement only served to enrage Tregear further. How could he ever have thought that she could replace Annabella? And that thought became the tipping point for his madness as he cried out his angry frustration, clawed at Eve's flesh, sucked her blood from the scratches and tears, ripped open her body with renewed vigour.

But why was she so passive? Why didn't she fight and scream or plead for her life like so many of his other victims had? Their fighting had intensified his passion and satisfaction on feeding, but she wouldn't even give him that. Instead she seemed oblivious to Tregear and the pain he caused her. Unfeeling. Her soul locked away somewhere beyond his reach, infuriating him even more. Weakened now, her body slumped to the concrete floor of the warehouse, yet she never uttered so much as a moan, cocooned by shock, her mind numbed to reality. She just stared back at the door through which they had come, waiting for her knight in shining armour to arrive to save her, passive and disconnected while Tregear drained the life from her. He'd wanted her to cry out, thrash about, call his name the way she'd done when he'd made love to her. She'd done none of that; and in denying him her passion had made his feasting unsatisfying.

Finally, his ravenous hunger quenched, his own senses heightened, Tregear lowered her inert body to the cold hard floor. Looking over Eve's still body he saw Annabella standing by a distant wall; a little shocked, a little frightened, but waiting to be noticed.

Self-consciously, he licked the blood away from his lips.

"Come," Tregear said, extending a hand to her in invitation. "I will make you my wife. Your love will be rewarded."

The staccato of her heels across the concrete floor was the only sound to be heard. There was no fear in her heart now; she knew that she'd do anything if it meant staying with Tregear.

He held her to him, tearing at his wrist until his blood ran freely. Annabella showed no hesitation as she drank his tainted blood and the heat of her nervous excitement gave him the satisfaction that Eve could not. He'd always sworn he'd never make another like himself, but also knew now that he couldn't bear to live without her.

"It won't make you any younger, but at least there'll be more time for us to be together."

"We can find others like her, young girls eager for well-paid easy work, a little adventure. We'll engage a few. I was wrong in appointing just the one. If we employ a few, we shouldn't encounter this problem again if one of them should decide to … leave us." Annabella glanced at the torn remains of Eve. Her sanguine face was almost comical, given her circumstances; as if by denying what had happened to her could have saved her. Stupid girl. Annabella felt no remorse, only something akin to victory. Tregear was hers once more.

"And you will feed off them as I have?" His question interrupted her reverie.

"If it means I continue to be with you," Annabella replied with quiet determination.

Tregear knew it was imperative that they not be seen leaving the murder site, and of course an alibi had to be established. That, at least, would be easier now that Annabella was his accomplice. They would simply vouch for each other.

In the distance Tregear thought he could hear the measured footfall of the security guard on his return route. A pre-dawn breeze caught a loose piece of roofing iron and it banged, capturing Tregear's attention. It had been many years since he'd made a leap that high, but it could be done, especially now that he was replete and infused with superhuman strength gained from his feasting. Even with the additional weight of Annabella in his arms he was confident he could make a safe and clueless exit.

It was a hot mid-day when the police arrived to ask their questions. Logically, the windows and plantation shutters were closed to keep in the cool.

Tregear was well-rehearsed in what to say. Annabella took the news with just the right hint of shocked sadness. Yes, she'd seen Eve leave the ball with Tregear, who had been angry; they'd had some falling out. She'd followed the couple to try to console them both, but Eve wouldn't listen to reason and she'd run off into the night. Annabella had come to the house with Tregear and had stayed with her good friend throughout the night and into the day.

How unfortunate that Eve had become a murder victim. If only she'd stayed with them she would have been safe. Had anyone bothered to question Eve's boyfriend, who'd seemed inordinately possessive of Eve and irritated with her being in Tregear's employ …?

A seed was planted. The police withdrew to take their enquiries elsewhere. Maybe the boyfriend would be blamed for her murder? Now wouldn't that be justice?

Tomorrow they'd design ads to sprinkle around the nearby university, calling for young women to provide occasional 'company' to a discerning couple.

I was close to Eve's age when I wrote 'Only Women Bleed'; now I'm closer to Annabella's. It's interesting having seen this story from both sides of the coin. On one level it's a vampire story, on another it's a love story. (But aren't all vampire stories love stories to some degree?)

'Only Women Bleed' was published in Harbinger *issue 2, 1999. Editor: Erika Lacey.*

That Ain't No Emu Egg

(published as Rocket and Sparky)

Our camel's name is Rocket. One previous owner, low kilometres, no spit, no bite, no buck. And all that's true, but I've got the hump because I always wanted a pony.

Rocket's saddle is double-barrelled, so I can steer the camel, and my little brother, Roy, can ride behind. I told my Dad you can ride double on a pony too. I've told him heaps of times, but all he does is look around our farm and ask me: what would a pony eat?

He has a point. He bought our 140 acres sight unseen, just going by some photos he'd been sent, saying it was too good to be true. That's because it was. There was long, lush grass and cattle grazing in those photos. Doesn't look like anything I've seen around here. Dad says the photos were taken in a good year. Good years must be few and far between, because we've been here three years now and all I've ever seen is spinifex and mulga, and rolling golden sand dunes that Rocket runs over easily.

The golden sand gave me an idea. There *must* be gold out here somewhere, maybe even a Lasseter's Reef. If we could just find it we'd be rich, and if we were rich we'd be able to buy a farm where there is some grass, then I could have a pony. What could be simpler?

"Let me down, let me down!" Roy demands from the saddle-seat behind me. "I need a toilet break!"

He *always* needs a toilet break when we're out riding Rocket on a prospecting trip. I blame all that red cordial he guzzles down his throat from the old canteen he ties to Rocket's saddle, pretending he's a great explorer.

"Can we go just a little further?" I try to persuade Roy, but he and his bladder won't be swayed. Maybe it's his bladder being swayed that caused the problem in the first place?

"Down now!" Roy decrees as if he is a Raj, Rocket an elephant and I'm a mahout.

Little brothers; what a pest!

"Kush, kush" I call to Rocket, flapping his reins like a pair of leather wings.

Rocket comes to a stop, complaining bitterly. He's obviously been enjoying his walk. I "kush" again, and amid more camel complaints, Rocket sinks ungainly to his knees.

Roy clambers off the back saddle seat, looks around and asks me: "So where's the nearest tree?"

As if I carry such things around in my pockets perhaps?

"About two kilometres back that way from memory, Roy," I tell him, hiking my thumb back the way we've come.

"I need some privacy," Roy declares indignantly.

"Go behind the camel."

Rocket complains loudly at my suggestion. He probably thinks it's bad enough that I treat him like a lumpy pony, but Roy treating him as a privacy screen is pushing the friendship a bit too far.

"Turn around then," Roy demands.

"Gladly." I turn away to give him his privacy, wondering if he'd notice if I poured his red cordial over the desert sands. It'd save the hassle of him filtering it first. I reach out experimentally for the old canteen.

"Hands off my canteen!" he declares.

So much for that idea. I kick idly at a few pebbles at my feet, wishing they were opals. Maybe there was some gold around here? As good a place as any to take a look, I guess.

There's the sound of a zip being closed up, then Roy announces, "I'm going exploring." He's lost in plumes of kicked-up sand by the time I turn around.

"You be careful!" I call after him, but I'm soon regarding the rocks nearby, leaving reclining Rocket to chew his cud and contemplate the universe, or whatever it is camels think about when they're sitting thinking.

Grains of quartz shine like specks of silver in a rock I pick up, but I'm not that easily fooled anymore. I need big arteries of quartz, with veins of gold running through them, or preferably solid gold nuggets lying around the place.

"Sis, sis! I've found an emu's egg!"

I frown to myself. It's not impossible, I suppose, but I haven't noticed that many emus around the place.

And as Roy comes shimmering through the heat haze towards me, I can tell whatever he's lugging is too big to be an emu's egg.

I've *seen* an emu egg: big, and green and carved, but nothing as big as what Roy's dragging towards me. It's half his height, and twice his width. Watching him carry it is like watching a cheetah carrying an antelope carcass, or an arid climate Emperor penguin shuffling a gigantic egg on his feet.

It wasn't gold, that's for sure. But did it have any value? A meteorite maybe? Can you sell them on e-Bay? Could it make enough for us to buy a farm with grass on it so I could have a pony?

It looks more like an egg than a meteor though, I see as Roy gets closer. But what sort of bird would lay something that big?

"I'm keeping it," Roy states. He's panting from his exertions as he rests the egg on the golden sand and reaches for his canteen bottle. I mentally draw a map of where all the nearest trees are on the way home.

"How do you propose we get it home?" I ask him.

"Rocket's got saddle bags."

He has, but I'm not sure the egg would fit in one.

"Dad will never let you keep it," I warn him.

"Dad doesn't need to know."

I wonder how many omelettes can you make with an egg that size? If we opened an omelette stand, could we sell enough to buy a farm somewhere else so I can have a pony?

"Help me get it into the saddle bag? Pleeease?"

So we huff and puff, and we wrangle and pull, and finally we got *most* of the egg into the saddle bag. Roy has to sit side-saddle, one leg hooked around the handlebar at the front of the saddle, one hand holding the strap of the saddle bag to keep the massive egg in.

Rocket complains about having to carry excess baggage as he gets to his feet before I have a chance to tell him to. He'll only complain more if I ask him to kneel down again, and I feel sorry for him, so I decide to lead him rather than expect him to carry me as well.

When we get home, Roy hides the egg in the chook shed. Heaven help any fox or goanna that tries to steal it.

I don't tell Dad. I don't have to. We're all sound asleep in our beds when the egg cracks open on the twelfth stroke of midnight, loud enough to wake us all up.

"Well, there goes my idea for an omelette stand," I mutter.

Dad stammers and stutters while Roy crows and struts around the chook shed like a proud new father. At least I'd been right when I'd said no bird could ever lay an egg that big.

Our dragon's name is Sparky. No previous owner, low kilometres, and he hasn't burned the chook shed down ... at least not yet. We fed him powdered milk at first, but it turns out he's also partial to BBQ chicken. Dad isn't impressed, but he's also too frightened to do anything about it, so Sparky's avoided a spanking … at least so far. If he keeps growing at this rate, I don't think anyone will dare try.

In less than twenty-four hours, he was as big as Rocket, and strong with it. I've had Rocket's saddle on him, and taken him for a ride. He can cover more territory with a few flaps of his leathery wings than Rocket can cover in an hour. But I still haven't found my Lasseter's Reef. Maybe tomorrow I'll fly him in another direction.

Roy insists on coming with me. According to him, Sparky's *his* dragon, but Sparky only lets me drive, so Roy has to be content with riding in the back seat of the camel saddle. He wears goggles and a weathered leather cap, and pretends he's an ace pilot when we fly. A collection of airsick bags is tied to his saddle handle bar next to his canteen, I notice, but he hasn't used any yet. He just throws up over the side.

It's a versatile thing, that camel saddle. I reckon that's what gave me the idea to offer camel rides and dragon rides. The choice is yours! You might just have to wait a few minutes while we change the saddle over. I reckon we've got the market cornered. This one's a winner for sure! When I've made heaps of money I'll buy a farm with some grass on it, and I'll finally get that pony.

Published in Worlds Next Door, *Fablecroft Press, 2010. Editor: Tehani Croft.*

This was just one of those stories that flowed out of me. It was there almost in its entirety, and I was just a channel helping it make its way on to the screen. (Damn, why can't they all be like that?)

Anyone who has spent more than five minutes in my company has probably realised getting a pony has been a life-long (and unfulfilled) quest.

Aliens Here

I wanted the dolphins to come in to the shore. You called them in for me, emitting a sonic whistle that I should have known no human voice—or mind, for that matter—could ever duplicate.

They swam into the shallows to greet us, looking to you as if you were an old friend. We took off our clothes in the moonlight and swam out to play with them. They swam up to you immediately, but took their time when approaching me, circling around and around while making up their minds before finally accepting me.

I remember the buoyancy of my body and spirit in the water. And the tingle of the dolphins' sonar as it bounced through me. I felt safe in the inky blackness of the water. The whole ocean seemed like a womb. I thought I could never feel so satisfied, so content.

The stars shone down upon us as we all touched and caressed. You and I laughed our delight, and soon the dolphins were mimicking us with their high-pitched voices, so it sounded like the whole sea was laughing.

Finally, when my fingers and toes were all wrinkly, you suggested that we return to land. So regretfully I left those happy sea-creatures, and regretfully I came out of the salty womb to be born again on land as my ancestors must have done thousands of generations before.

As if denying part of what we were, we put our clothes back on.

The night was still and warm, and I could not find words to thank you enough for the joy you had given me. Yet I knew so little of you; a name, a phone number—not much more. But when we met I accepted you completely—just the way the dolphins did. It was as if you had always been a shadow in my life, as if you had walked every step with me, only I had never noticed until we met.

You took my hand as we walked along the shore. The dolphins followed us, but at a safe depth. We didn't talk too often, there was no need to. I wondered if this was love we'd fallen into? It had none of the usual trappings: no fast beating heart, no anxious glances, no constant groping from one to the other to reassure one's self with love's caresses.

It was deep, the bond we shared. It was instant depth from the very beginning. No discovering steps showing the way into each other's soul. Ours was just immediate bonding.

Never had I been so happy, so satisfied with my lot. Never even had I expected to be. Surely there was nothing that I had with any other man that came close to what I felt with you.

But in my mind one question lingered. A simple thing, no harm in asking.

"Ask me," you invited, as if you'd heard me say it. You didn't even break your stride.

"Tell me where you came from?" I ventured.

You stopped then, turning out to sea and looking skyward.

"You see that star?" You pointed to one that shone more brightly than its neighbours.

I nodded; reality hadn't struck yet.

"You call it Supernova 1987A. It used to be my star, my home."

My hand squeezing yours was a conciliatory gesture. "I'm sorry," I offered in a quiet voice, aware that no words of solace could ever be enough, but there didn't seem much else to say.

So you're an alien here? I thought. So what? Aren't we all?

Published in Under Magellanic Clouds, *Issue 4, Winter/ Spring 1998. Editor: Marijke Fitzgerald.*

Space Cow

She sighed at the slight sucking tug at her breast. It was not unpleasant. The weight of the lithe body upon her was not discomforting, nor was the warm wetness of the mouth that suckled from her.

It was times like these that she found herself almost overcome by a usually well-controlled maternal instinct. She actually half-wished that she could have a child. But a child was costly and would only be a hindrance to someone who wanted to see as much of the galaxy as possible in a lifetime.

Now the sucking stopped. Contented, her lessor got up, moved to the panoramic window to watch the first sun set for the evening. Its companion would follow in a few more hours time.

"It's not a bad place, here," Amorgan commented, wiping droplets of her milk away from his lips. "But I'll be glad to move on tomorrow."

"So will I," she replied. Time was a finite commodity and she didn't appreciate the type of traveller who wanted to spend years investigating every nook and cranny, every bit of new technology and architectural ruin of every planet they came across. There was a limit to how many beautiful historic buildings she could appreciate before they all started blurring into one. Fortunately Amorgan wasn't this type of traveller. Even when he found a planet he really liked, he could only manage to stay a space month or two, take in a short list of the most important things before he was itching to get back into space again. He was star-struck like no other she had ever known. He had to keep travelling. His need to see new planets, different parts of the galaxy almost matched her own.

She had been with Amorgan for the past two years and they got along well together. She had been leased to him, or at least her mammaries had (she just went along for the ride). She had two of the finest breasts around and she was proud of them. They were naturally large and firm, and kept unnaturally ripe. Once a week she took a soluble tablet that kept her producing milk for him, and twice a day he would drink from her. Her milk kept him alive, thriving, no matter what planet they were on, or what part of the galaxy they were transiting through.

Amorgan was a delicate creature with a specialised constitution. There were few foods on even fewer planets that he could actually eat that would benefit him. Some foods he could ingest, but not process to gain their nutrients, but many more he was allergic to, which meant he had to take his food supply with him wherever he travelled. When he'd started out, he had carted processed pills with him from planet to planet, but hadn't anticipated the ways they could become problematic. Government agencies were suspicious of his life support, thinking him to be some drug smuggler, even though he had no criminal record and his permits were correct and in order.

Then there'd been the problem of re-supply, or rather the lack of it. He'd almost starved to death several times waiting for a shipment of pills to arrive as some space freighter was delayed or rerouted somewhere lightyears away from him. Finally he had decided to take the plunge and change from pills to a 'feeding servant' to fulfil his nutritional needs. Such a servant could be leased from various agencies, and would travel with him so his energy source was always close at hand. Some of the servants could be purchased outright, but they weren't all as strikingly beautiful as Amorgan thought this companion was, and she was only available to lease.

She had the prerequisites needed for the position; she had an enhanced immune system that allowed her to safely eat a much wider range of foodstuffs than he could. She'd also had a subcutaneous filtering system calibrated to his specific needs so she wasn't passing contaminants on to him. Though he didn't see her large breasts as necessarily a part of her beauty, they produced a good supply of rich milk that would keep him fed. He wasn't concerned that his diet was monotonous; it was the price he gladly paid in order to travel to many planets, which was far more important to him. She shared his yearning for travel and adventure, and apart from the practicalities of their relationship, the journey was enhanced by having someone to share the trip. It was that much better for having someone to turn to and say, "Will you look at that? Have you ever seen anything like it? Well, I never!"

He offered his semblance of a smile to her and she returned it.

So here they were, sharing a symbiotic relationship, a frail little alien and his food supplier, both keen to explore the galaxy.

'Space Cow' was published in the Melbourne University Science Fiction Association magazine yggdrasil, *1983 Issue 1. Editors: Bruce Alan Fraser and Clive Newall.*

I think 'Space Cow' and 'Only Women Bleed' are twinned, written as an act of rebellion. Like a pre-programmed computer, the human body comes as a set package. You can't pick and choose what bits you want, that are likely to be most useful for your specific needs, (though more and more of late you can reformat your package and get upgrades if you can afford to.) I was fairly sure from an early age that I didn't want to have children, so the children-making bits were superfluous to my needs. (The bits for sex turned out to be useful, but I would have gladly done away with all the swings and roundabouts of the monthly cycle—and found another excuse for craving chocolate!) I've found other uses for parts of the human anatomy, and no, I've never been tempted to write a story about an appendix.

When I uncovered my contributor's copy of yggdrasil, I was rather surprised to find the other person with fiction in that issue was Sean McMullen, who went on to gain great acclaim as a spec fic writer. Also in that issue was Part 1 of a transcript of a talk Douglas Adams gave at Melbourne University in late 1982 (q.v.). I was compelled to purchase the next issue so I could read the rest of the Douglas Adams transcript. By that stage, Sean McMullen had taken over as editor.

She Just Dropped In

There were those who still argued that it was a costly and fruitless exercise to send men into space to explore the planets. Items of equipment—satellites, landers, on-board cameras, computers— were expendable, they argued. Human beings were not. (Besides, while technology was getting smaller, cheaper to manufacture and more efficient, human beings were actually getting larger.)

Then there was the other school of thought which claimed that man could not conquer the other planets in the solar system, or beyond, by remote control. There had to be a human being right there, along with all the technology and machinery, to put their bootprint on the alien ground to make it all more real, less distant, less sterile. Besides, it gave a space mission a sense of danger, and heroics, when someone's mortality—or immortality—was also on the line.

The Roman Empire had fallen centuries before, but life was still about bread and circuses. Give them what they wanted and the masses would support anything. Think of the publicity, the flood of funding, the renewed interest in space exploration if they could put a man on Mars!

But there had to be compromises. Budgets were restricted. They could only afford to send one man on the mission. It would have to be a special man, one who could tolerate the cold loneliness of outer space for long drafts of time without any undue psychological effect. A man who would return to Earth as a hero—or who could be held aloft as a hero if he didn't return.

The best of the best were called from around the world: America, Russia, China, India, France, Japan all sent selected candidates. If there were rich individuals who could contribute financially to the program, and who thought they were made of the Right Stuff for such a perilous mission, their applications were also accepted. Their wallets were milked on the understanding that you can pay to be a hero, and in the secret knowledge that you don't send billionaires on potentially dangerous space missions, despite how good the PR looked. One by one, the candidates were all vetted out gently, so in the end only the finest astronauts—those with some experience with space travel—were left to battle it out amongst themselves. Of those it came down to Kreshenko and Popov from Russia, Chen from China, and Hetherington from the United States as finalists.

By rights, by test results alone, it should have been Kreshenko who got the coveted ride. But the American selectors tipped the scales in their favour.

Those who knew him said that Hetherington deserved to be the one to go. Cold-hearted, solitary bastard that he was, he'd be perfectly at home in a tin-can hurtling towards Mars, content in his splendid isolation. With his short-cropped ice-blond hair and perfect teeth he'd look great in all the publicity photos, even if his distant demeanour was a little off-putting.

Trying to show no ill-will towards him, his team-mates took Hetherington out for drinks on his last night before leaving the planet, thinking if they couldn't get into space themselves, the next best thing was to give him the mother of all hangovers to take with him.

Hetherington let them buy him drinks until he'd drunk most of them under the table. Only Kreshenko was left standing—

well, he was upright, if swaying and bleary-eyed, as Hetherington picked up his coat and a strange blonde woman who had been discreetly waiting for him in the background at the bar most of the night.

"There goes the luckiest bastard I've ever met." Kreshenko's accent had become thicker, his speech more slurred, as the night had progressed. "And I thought that space was the only lady good enough for him. Salute, Tovarich!"

With that, Kreshenko gulped the dregs of his vodka from his shot glass before collapsing unceremoniously across the table they'd been sitting at.

To varying degrees, they all nursed hangovers the next morning, probably even Hetherington, yet of all of them he seemed the least worse for wear. He was his usual icy-cool, precise, methodical self as he went through his final debriefing and the other three astronauts watched on with varying degrees of envy and hate in their eyes.

He'd been selected as Mr Perfect, and they'd all come so close to being him.

The earth-bound three stood together to watch as the Mars launch went off without a hitch. Then Chen turned and bowed to his Russian colleagues, explaining that now the eyes of the world were elsewhere, he'd been summoned back to China urgently to participate in a program for the China National Space Administration and was leaving right away.

Kreshenko turned to Popov after Chen had left them. "He'll be on his way to Mars before you know it, mark my words," he told his colleague.

Popov made a noise of agreement. "But do you think they have a faster rocket, and will they send him off now? Or will they wait to see if Hetherington makes it back unscathed first?"

That was a mystery, but neither of them had any doubts China had a rocket at the ready. There'd be no such reprise for them. Both had been given permission to stay at the launch site for the first few weeks of Hetherington's mission, to make themselves available for interviews and other publicity opportunities. (Fortunately, by the grace of God, or some higher authority, there'd been no media following them when they'd all gone for their farewell drinks with Hetherington in the bar.)

"Should we go back to our hotel, do you think? Their restaurant should still be open." Popov, who had to watch his weight all the way through the selection period, was always thinking of food. Only now, sure that he wouldn't be on this mission or any other in the near future, could he indulge his fantasies.

"Let's make our presence known to Mission Control first. Someone from the media might want to ask us our opinion."

"Alright, I'll buy a chocolate bar at the vending machine then," Popov said, already fishing through his pockets for change, not noticing the look of derision Kreshenko had thrown him. They wandered to the Control Room for a quick reconnoitre.

It seemed the whole world, or pretty close to it, had watched the take-off and was tracking the progress of the mission, hanging on every report Hetherington sent back home; at least for the first few days. Then interest began to wane and the ratings began to drop off after that; there was a new political debacle to grab their attention.

For the first two weeks the two Russians made daily visits to Mission Control, but there were fewer and fewer reporters there now and as the media interest ebbed so did their enthusiasm.

Watching Hetherington go through the same routines they'd all trained for hundreds, if not thousands of times before, wasn't much fun for the two 'also-rans'.

"Makes you think how bored we would get if it was one of us, eh?" Popov asked his comrade as they watched Hetherington on the big screen in Mission Control.

"If it was me up there, I promise you I would be anything but bored," Kreshenko replied. "Being in space is like being in the arms of a lover to me. Every time I go up. *Every* time! I never tire of it, I could stay up there forever."

"Maybe there'll be other missions," Popov offered him small solace. "You might still get there one day."

"Only if our Chinese colleague needs a co-pilot, which I doubt he does." He said this quietly in Russian, even though it was an open secret; and even though more of the staff in Control spoke Russian than were letting on. The world had no place to hide secrets any more.

Popov turned his attention to the woman at the nearest computer monitor. "How's everything going on the mission?" he asked her conversationally.

Chocolate wrappers and congealing dregs in the coffee cup at her post said it all before she could put it into words.

"It's been a quiet shift, with more of the same expected," Bea answered him.

"And our hero?" Kreshenko enquired, watching him on the viewscreen.

"Performing to perfection, or course," Bea responded. She was glad they'd decided to stop at her monitoring station. At this stage in her shift, she'd welcome any distraction. (And the journey had just started! They all had months just like this before them. Except for the Russians. They'd be leaving soon to take up other duties.)

For a while the three of them continued to watch Hetherington on the big screen, made conversation about his biometrics, before discussing the weather outside the walls of Mission Control and the chances of the two teams in the football game.

It wasn't long before Popov became distracted. Kreshenko could read his body language like a book.

"The cafeteria should be open, yes? Is it too early for lunch, do you think?" Popov asked.

Kreshenko rolled his eyes, muttered "Bozhe moi" to himself. Popov's over-eating to compensate for missing out on the Mars mission was being noticed, and commented on by others now, too. It was embarrassing Kreshenko. He thought the subsidised meals they sold at the Mission Control canteen were the only reason Popov was keen to come to Mission Control every day. The man was running to fat.

Kreshenko was just about to suggest that Bea might like to join them when Hetherington's voice over the relay diverted his attention.

"What are you doing here?" Hetherington asked, sounding surprised and looking at something off-camera.

"His voice has changed," Kreshenko noticed. Hetherington usually spoke in a controlled, neutral, clipped voice with all hints of his normal southern drawl supressed. It was only when he was really relaxed—and that took quite a number of drinks to achieve, Kreshenko knew—that he'd let his guard drop and get that twang in his voice.

Even Popov was alert to the change. "What did he say?"

Bea and half a dozen other mission monitors were exchanging puzzled glances, checking their computer screens, donning headsets to hear Hetherington without distraction, make sure they hadn't misheard, or got interference from somewhere else.

The Mission Controller came out of his stupor, prowled the control room like a tiger. "Heads up, people! Bea, talk to our man. Let's see why he's suddenly slipped into party mode."

Kreshenko glanced appraisingly at the Mission Controller. He hadn't been to any of their off-base recreational activities, but he must have got a good understanding of all the final candidates.

"Hetherington, this is Mission Control. Please acknowledge," Bea spoke into the microphone of her headset, then she waited, unaware of her lips moving as she quietly counted the seconds off to herself. It would take a while for the message to relay. All they could do was watch and wait.

"May I suggest you run an analysis of the cabin atmosphere?" Kreshenko suggested.

The Mission Controller picked up his words. "Good idea. Raymond, run atmosphere diagnostics. Let's see what Hetherington's breathing."

"His biometrics looked fine last time we ran them."

"Well run them *again*." There was a 'not on my shift' edge to the Mission Controller's voice.

"Yeah, of course I remember that last night in the bar, honey." Hetherington's attention was still fixated on something off-screen.

"He's hallucinating," Popov opined. "Has anyone called the Mission doctor? He should be seeing this."

"Command the camera to do a 360 view of the cabin. Let's see what he's looking at," the Controller asked one of the observers. There was a staccato of computer keys.

"Say what? You want to do what?" Hetherington drawled as he gave a big toothy smile.

"Atmosphere mix and pressure in the cabin reads as normal, sir," one of the controllers reported. "Hetherington's biometrics report a slight elevation in heartbeat and blood pressure, but still within acceptable ranges.

"Of all the fucking times for Mr Cool to lose his marbles!" the Mission Controller muttered angrily before talking into the mike on his headset. "Hetherington? Dammit, Hetherington, talk to us!"

But Hetherington was only interested in talking to someone in real time apparently.

As they watched the large screen, they all heard as Bea's words were broadcast through the cabin's speakers. Hetherington showed no response to their request.

"Dammit, where's that doctor?" the Mission Controller snarled.

"His biometrics still registering as normal, sir. Nothing abnormal about his brainwave activity either." The information was scrolling down the main screen.

The on-board cameras received their orders and panned around the cockpit.

Just for a second, Kreshenko thought he saw a helmeted face at the viewport as the camera panned past. A woman's face, that of the woman who'd waited for Hetherington in the bar that last night. But no, it must have been his imagination playing tricks on him. Though he itched to say, "Go back, look at that," he kept silent. He'd look more closely when the camera did its next sweep.

"Not so perfect after all?" Popov murmured to his countryman as they watched the drama progress.

"It could happen to anyone," Kreshenko reminded him. "But what lousy timing."

The Mission Controller's voice kept rising in pitch as he tried to get Hetherington to acknowledge him, but the astronaut seemed oblivious to their calls.

"Shit, where's he heading now? Track the camera! Track the camera!"

"He's moving towards the airlock, sir."

"Send an override command to lock it," the Mission Controller snapped.

"Do you hear that knocking?" Kreshenko asked Popov privately.

The other man shrugged noncommittally. "It could be anything. Anything at all."

But it wasn't consistent, and if didn't sound like part of the ship or a malfunction in part of the on-board technology. They'd all been trained to recognise unusual noises.

"But you'd agree it's not coming from inside the ship?" Kreshenko pressed him, speaking Russian.

Popov gave a shrug, answered in Russian. "To you, yes. To an official board of enquiry, no. This mission is going belly-up, big time. Look at the Mission Controller, he's shitting himself. He wasn't trained to deal with anything like this. Makes me glad I wasn't chosen to go after all."

You'd be bored and over-eating all your food rations, Kreshenko thought, but didn't say anything to Popov.

"Come on in, honey. I'll just get the door for you."

"He's trying to open the airlock."

It took only a quick calculation to realise the remote command to lock down the airlock wouldn't have reached the ship yet.

Popov looked away from the screen on the pretence of checking his pockets for coins, while Kreshenko couldn't tear his eyes away from the slow-moving drama unfolding before them, trying to catch another view of the phantom woman he thought he'd seen outside the ship to vindicate his sanity. The woman who'd lured Hetherington out of the bar that night, he'd seen her, he was sure of it! The woman who seemed to be luring him to his death now.

"Hetherington! Don't open that damned door!" the Mission Controller yelled into his mike.

"Too late, Controller," Kreshenko said quietly. The command to lock the airlock should have reached the ship by now, but the vision they were watching was a couple of minutes old. "He's already dead."

Published in Vile Temptress, *2000. Editor: Zara Baxter.*

Party

(as it appeared in *Antipodean SF* Issue 1)

It was a party to celebrate the (white) Australian dream. I'd taken a redundancy package, bought a few acres and a rundown farmhouse out the back of beyond.

Saved two donkeys and a clydesdale from the knackery. They'd do for company.

I'd only sent out a few invitations. Didn't expect anyone much to show except for a few loyal friends.

Everybody came. And brought their friends, family and strangers they'd met somewhere along the way, or at least that was how it seemed.

Fortunately food and drink were no problem. Everyone brought something. We had a spit roast, heaps of salad, tonnes of bread, cheese, beer and wine.

My ex-flatmate, Bean, was there. The mad-keen war-gamer who'd bought a dragon egg at a con once. Cute idea until it hatched. Cute dragon until it grew, then Bean and the dragon moved way out west. Both work for the Department of National Parks and Wildlife these days, flaming feral pigs. I didn't like the way the dragon was eyeing my donkeys though. I hoped it had been fed recently.

I spent the night running around, fussing over food and drinks, catching snippets of conversation.

At least there'd be no problem with gate-crashers, I thought, taking time out to stare at the stars that hung like ripe plums in the sky.

"Oh shit, no!" I cried as one of those stars descended and landed in the back paddock. "Who invited them?"

"Err … I did," Bean said behind me, as pale, almond eyed, dome headed aliens disembarked from their craft, and mingled with the other party goers.

"Quick, hide the Coca-Cola. You know how wild those guys get when they go on a bender!"

The beer drinkers got drunk and fell asleep around the fire. The wine drinkers and the non-boozers disappeared into my hay-loft to talk, or else went to explore the space ship.

I—as usual—found myself alone, in the kitchen, with all that washing up to be done. No one else was going to volunteer to do it. Bastards!

As I muttered bitterly to myself, immersed up to the elbow in soap suds, one of the shorter aliens walked silently into the kitchen, picked up a tea-towel and started drying.

"At least there's one gentleman here," I said, though they didn't seem to bother with genders.

He (if it was a 'he') looked up at me and blinked—their standard form of communication.

The washing up finally completed, I ferreted in the fridge, producing two hidden cans of Coke.

"Hope you're old enough to be drinking this stuff," I said handing a can to my helper.

I wandered out to the hillock, the alien following after me. We sat in companionable silence watching one last star fade from the sky, bowing gracefully to morning.

'Party' was published in Antipodean SF *Issue 1 (1998). Editor: Ion Newcombe.*
When Nuke threw down the challenge to write flash fiction, stories of 500 words or less, I thought it couldn't be done, but I had to give it a try, and 'Party' was my first effort. Writing flash fiction taught me to cut back to the bare essentials, only using what was important to tell the story—useful skills to have. Antipodean SF *has gone from strength to strength, and has given lots of writers an important venue to get their work exposed to an appreciative reading public.*

The Dragon Ring

My grandfather was a strange old man. I liked him a lot. My brothers, all older than me, for I am the youngest as well as being the only girl, used to grumble on the rare occasions we visited him as children. I liked visiting my grandfather and his house much more than the boys ever did. Grandfather probably suspected as much by the reluctant way they entered his house and the eager way they left it.

He lived alone, or at least we always presumed so, in a small house that was cluttered with fascinating paraphernalia. It was a warm, welcoming house. I could have spent hours and days exploring it if given a chance. He had some interesting things there, many delicate and fragile, but he was not averse to letting little hands explore them, just as long as the owners of the hands knew how to respect the object; because if you respect something you'll never hurt or break it.

Grandfather always managed to treat children like short adults instead of patronising them the way so many adults do.

He was not at all averse to talking to things like trees, birds, cats and dogs. He talked to them all in the same way that he talked to children: as if they were equals too. While I delighted in this, feeling that it gave me permission to hold long conversations with anything and everything I chanced across, my brothers would take great joy in speculating on my grandfather's sanity.

There was always something with my grandfather, a something called 'Kaliyat' that Grandfather talked of, at, and sometimes to. One of my brothers mistook the name for 'Alleycat' and argued that it was a cat Grandfather had owned at some stage or another. Another brother supposed that perhaps it was a pet name for Grandma, who had died before any of us were born. Maybe he thought he was talking to her ghost? But our parents dismissed all our theories and the mystery remained unsolved.

Whatever or whoever this Kaliyat was, it still seemed to crave his attention. My grandfather would sometimes interrupt conversations to chide it with a gruff "Not now!" or "Wait until I've finished talking!" as if it was an impatient child tugging at his sleeve, trying to get noticed. Yet at other times I'd hear him sing to it and murmur reassurances.

Kaliyat enjoyed walks in the park as much as I did, it seemed. To entertain us both, Grandpa would indulge me (and presumably Kaliyat) in long walks there after lunch. He would talk to me of philosophy—though I didn't know it was philosophy then. And he would show me the treasures of the world: a fallen leaf in winter with all the green eaten away so that only the network of brown veins remained—a skeleton of the beauty that once was, but beautiful and perfect in its own way; an industrious caterpillar in springtime; a gecko in summer. The creature ran into the palm of his hand when he called it. I thought it was magic.

He taught me to respect and take pleasure in all the simple things that my brothers ignored, or destroyed in their boisterous pursuits.

Sometimes we'd find real treasures. We found a gold bracelet under some fallen leaves once. My grandfather went straight to the spot as if he was guided. When he was unable to locate the owner he gave the bracelet to me. I marvelled at how the rectangular gold links sparkled in the sun.

My grandfather wore no jewellery of his own, save for a bulky silver ring. It was carved in the shape of a sleeping dragon. I could never picture my grandfather without that ring, though I never really paid that much attention to it. It was always there, that was all. A blur of silver when he moved his hand, an extra, metal, knuckle when his hand was still.

As I grew up, my mother often lamented what a shame it was that little girls stop being little girls. She was my grandfather's only daughter and I was hers.

When Grandfather died, he left me a fortune. A fool's fortune, my brothers all jeered. They did not mourn his death as I did. They were glad to be rid of the social embarrassment an eccentric old man was to them.

I inherited his friendly little house and all that was in it: his stuffed eagle, wings outstretched, glass eyes blazing with fury so you always expected it to screech at you; his brass telescope, barometer, collection of rocks, minerals and shells; the old wooden rocking-horse, my childhood steed salvaged from the garbage tip and lovingly restored; his books, some with leather covers; his cufflinks; and a history in photos. Most importantly— and this he stated categorically in his will—I was to become the sole owner of his dragon ring.

"Old junk," my brothers all sneered, but they had been his treasures and I had inherited them gratefully.

What a waste, they lamented under their breaths, that Grandfather's house should come intact to me, rather than being sold off to line their pockets.

His old house welcomed me, as it had always done when I visited him. (For unlike my brothers, my visits had gone on past my childhood.) There was no cold ghost to haunt me from this place, just a warm glow to let me feel I belonged in his house.

The dragon ring I put in the place of honour on the mantelpiece in the loungeroom. There I left it, thinking it was too big, both in band-size and in bulk, for me to wear.

On my first night there I did wonder if I would now get to meet dear old Kaliyat. Or had he followed my grandfather into the nether world? But I heard no voices, so I paid no mind … not for the first night at least.

I can't say exactly when I first noticed it, but there was to be heard in that house a very quiet whimpering. It was never consistent. It would start then stop, only to start again later. At first I assumed it was a neighbour's dog, though they had no dog. Then I thought it was merely the wind howling through the nearby trees, though there was no wind. Finally, I traced the sound through the house to the loungeroom, and eventually to the mantelpiece and the dragon ring.

"Kaliyat?" I wondered aloud.

Immediately the crying stopped, as a puppy will stop whimpering when you call its name.

I touched the metal form of the sleeping dragon, expecting to feel a cool metallic sensation. I was surprised to feel the silver was warm.

Could it have been the ring my Grandfather had talked to all these years?

I thought back to a conversation we'd had many years ago. It was the only time my grandfather had spoken of the ring, saying that the ring had been specially carved for him by a wise old man in China, and that it had great power.

Then he said that when he died I was to have the ring. I was to snatch it from his cold, stiff fingers if I had to, to stop my greedy brothers squabbling over who would hock it, sell it for scrap metal or melt it down. It was never to be sold or melted down, Grandfather impressed upon me.

Now I stroked the ring gently, fingers running over the intricately carved scales. I felt a gentle tingle through my fingertips in response. The ring seemed pleased by my company. When I stopped my caresses it whined again, so I picked it up and put it on my finger. I felt a warmth spread up my hand as the silver dragon ring expressed its pleasure.

"Kaliyat," I whispered to the ring and felt its presence surround and embrace me.

Finally, I knew what Kaliyat was.

From there I learned the ring's language, for it did communicate in its own way. I experienced for myself Kaliyat's habit of interrupting conversations. To get my attention, it would increase the intensity of the tingling in my fingers until the demand became annoying. It wasn't long before I found myself sharply telling it to be patient.

If it craved fresh air, the ring would pull towards the nearest open window or door. It seemed to suffer from claustrophobia at times; and I think I took it for more scenic walks than Grandfather ever did.

The ring's method of divining led me to a few earthly fortunes. By letting Kaliyat lead the way, I would often come across lost money and jewellery. I was able to reunite some of it with its rightful owners by scouring 'lost and found' columns in the local papers, or turning it in to the police, often to get it back when it went unclaimed.

Kaliyat was an amicable enough companion. The only objection the ring had to anything was its phobia to dogs. If a dog barked at me, I could feel the metal slink up my finger, trying to get away, and I could almost hear the dragon hiss its fear.

When I wore the ring, I had cause to talk to things just as my grandfather had. And they had cause to answer me.

The first time the stuffed eagle in the hallway screeched, as I'd always expected it to, I leapt in terror. Fortunately it screeches very rarely. Like most of the other paraphernalia in the house, the eagle is content to be admired and respected, but they all enjoy being noticed and talked to from time to time, just like people do.

With so much activity in my life, I never found a desire, a need, or even the time to bother about marriage, which is probably just as well.

My brothers, one by one discovering I'd acquired Grandfather's habit of talking to things, and especially to Kaliyat, one by one stopped visiting their little sister. They all got married and had children, but they never sent their children to visit their aunt. I suppose they feared I'd bewitch them, as they thought I was bewitched by Grandfather. Though I think that their shame keeps them a little from me as well. It's not so much that they fear I'm a madwoman. They know I'm not. I think it's more guilt left over from their childhood when they had no time or patience to spend pleasant hours with our grandfather the way I did.

So I've grown old alone, and they've grown older without me.

There is no one in my family to give the dragon ring to, so when it eventually comes my turn to die, (and don't worry, I don't plan to do so for some time yet!) I want you to have my Kaliyat and his warm, friendly little house.

I leave you these things because you have walked with me, and you have talked to me, and you have not abandoned me when I called to Kaliyat, or when I've talked to other things. And you've heard my story through.

Remember me a little, and don't be sad when I depart. Just promise me you'll never hock this ring or have it melted down, for this ring will have none of that.

My grandfather was a strange old man.

'The Dragon Ring' received an Honourable Mention in the Mary Grant Bruce Awards in 1985. It was published in Harbinger, *Issue 1, 1999. Editor: Erika Lacey.*

HG

She was in a hospital. Her mind knew it was a hospital before her recalcitrant mouth could say the word. She hated hospitals!

The nursing staff talked to her as if she was an infant. Perhaps she was? Perhaps she was new born? Dreams, memories and images came to her, and it was hard to define one reality from another at first; all were blurred, mixed … muddy.

They spoke one word to her that almost made sense, repeated it so she came to understand she was no babe fresh to the earth. Stroke. You've had a stroke, love. But you're safe now. We'll make you well again.

But she had her doubts.

At first she thought he was a doctor, hovering as he did at the edge of her vision. But the doctors spoke to her (brusquely, briefly) and talked to the nurses (sometimes rudely) before hurrying away.

He didn't hurry away, but he didn't speak either. He just hovered, shyly, at the edge of her vision, and seemed to study her.

Memories unfolded slowly like the petals of a flower. Those you loved, didn't they come to you as you died to escort you to the next world? That sounded right … but he was no one she could remember. Why would they send a stranger to escort her to the after-life?

She spat words like a toddler, had to learn to speak again, identify things, turn words into sentences, make herself understood. The well-trained nursing staff were patient, encouraging, even sympathetic to her frustrations on the bad days when progress, like a landslide, pushed her backwards instead of the way she wanted to go. On those days, she'd turn her attention to him, her guardian angel, and focus on him with the same intensity that he studied her.

What are you waiting for? her mind screamed at him. *If you've come to escort me to whatever comes after this, take me now! How much more humiliation do I have to suffer?*

"What is it, love?" the nurse asked with a smile, knowing her mind had strayed off their session.

A skinny arm, from which blood still oozed because they couldn't get the dose of anti-coagulants right, shook as she tried to point feebly at her silent observer. Carefully, as she had been trained to, she tasted each part of each word she wanted to speak, as if it was ripe fruit. "Can ... you ... see him ... too?"

The nurse looked over her shoulder, acknowledged her Guardian Angel with another warm smile. They weren't *supposed* to do that, were they? She expected the nurse to say, "Yes love, that's the one who'll escort you away from here when you die. We get a lot of them around the terminal ward. Won't be long now." But the nurse didn't address her at all. Instead she said, "It's alright. Come closer if you want."

And shyly, hesitantly, he did.

The gentlest smile curved his lips upward as he looked down at her. "Hello, my love."

My love, he'd said. Not just "love", the generic title the nurses used. My love, as if it were personal. And the look in his eyes said that she meant a lot to him. But who was he?

"How are you feeling?" he asked her, as he tentatively touched her hair.

"Like ..." Oh damn it all, what had she begun to say? It was like trying to catch a fish with your bare hands sometimes! Not in a barrel, but swimming in the ocean. You plunged your hand into your vocabulary and all the words just skittered away!

But he was looking at her anxiously, expectantly. Clear grey eyes, a rarity these days. She tried again.

"Like ... I've been ..." *Put the words together, make the connection, make the connection!* "... hit by a bus." Yes, that was it, dredged up from somewhere in her grey matter, the last spoken all in a rush. That's what she'd wanted to tell him.

And he smiled, and stroked her hair again, and she thought she'd walk through hell in her bare feet to see that smile again ... but why couldn't she remember him?

"You're doing very well." His words were a breeze tickling her on a hot summer's day.

"Take ... me ... home," she implored, though she had no idea if she meant her spiritual home or her physical home. Did she have a physical home? She must belong somewhere. Another door was unlocked, a slide presentation of rooms cascaded through her head. Winter sunlight spilled like runny cheese into a room with a desk and leatherbound books. Something comfortable stirred within her.

"Of course, my love; when you're better."

"You're well on your way," the nurse reassured her, and she nodded and tried to stifle a yawn, for she was suddenly very tired.

"You've had a busy day," the nurse told her.

He took the nurse's hint. "Catch up on your sleep," he suggested, and he bent to kiss her lightly on her brow. Her heart fluttered at this simple caress. She had no doubt now that he loved her ... but who was he?

She closed her eyes, imagined her mind as a computer, tried to get the relays to interconnect, make the web that freed the memory. He must be in there somewhere! But why couldn't she remember?

The night nurse's name was ... Margaretta? No. Mary? No. Maria? Yes! She was married, and had three children: a boy and two girls. Yes, her mind could unscramble and work normally sometimes.

And her own name was Grace. Or so they told her. It sounded familiar, right. Like the room with the sunlight like runny cheese, it suited her.

She knew she had a dog and cat waiting for her back home, and that she drove a ... that she drove a ... oh, bother, what was it again? Her car. An electric/solar hybrid called a ...? Called a ...? Think of the dog. Blob, no, Bob. Think of taking Bob to the beach. He jumps into the back of the *Tesla*. Yes, that was it, she drove a Tesla. Amazing how her brain worked out its own detours, sometimes took the scenic route, but got her there in the end ...

She pictured the cat sitting on her lap, could feel its warm weight on a cold winter's day. An overfed tabby, sleek and content. And the cat's name was ... Frog? Molly? Matty? Mog! The cat's name was Mog. They'd be missing her right now. Who was feeding them? Playing with them? Surely he'd be doing that, wouldn't he? But no matter how hard she tried, why couldn't she grasp some hint of him in her memory, the way she could with her dog and cat? The way she could with the night nurse's name? Who had drilled a hole in her brain and sucked all memory of him out?

After that introduction he was not so shy. No longer hovering at the periphery of her vision, he would loiter by her bed, help her dress, attend the physio sessions with her, cheering her on. Buoyed by his angel wings she made a good recovery: reclaiming her mobility, her power of speech, her memories, save the one of who he was. Finally she decided the specific amnesia didn't matter. He was in her life now, and felt so comfortable there that he must have spent a long time as her familiar, close at hand.

The doctors and nurses were all pleased with her progress. They'd got the mix of anti-coagulants right so she no longer leaked blood, and she was infused with a cocktail of hitch-hikers? ... parasites? ... road-cleaners? A microscopic workforce that swept through her veins carrying out repair work, reinforcing thin walls, keeping the platelets moving along, making sure clots didn't form. Nanobots!

Finally they gave her the all clear and he offered her his arm to steady her as he took her home.

She remembered her home from the slideshow that had rotated through her brain. Warm, welcoming, filled with hope and love and dreams. She was keen to get back into her house, pat her dog and stroke her cat again.

"Take your time," he warned her as she stumbled up the steps, using the newly installed handrail to haul herself towards the shut front door.

There was a security keypad by the door, but she hadn't even thought of the access code and couldn't remember it now. She began to get worried. Another memory sprung to meet her, "Keys!" she cried out anxiously. Keys would let her in if she couldn't remember the access code. "I've forgotten my keys!"

"I have them here. Just wait on the top step."

He gently manoeuvred her out of the way and unlocked the door while she fidgeted, excited as a child on Christmas morning. She tried to sneak past him, but he lifted her up in his arms and carried her across the threshold like a grey-haired bride. "Welcome home, my love," he whispered in her ear as he lowered her down, holding her arm as she stood on unsteady legs and looked around her.

One open doorway beckoned to her more strongly than all the others down the hall. Following her instincts she found herself standing in the room where the winter sunlight fell like golden cheese. The room smelled of dust, as if—like her mind—it had been shut up for too long.

And there was the large old ... no, antique ... wooden desk, polished to a deep brown hue and smelling faintly of beeswax, the laptop closed on top of it. Her fingers itched to open it, to return to the tools of her trade. She had long ago remembered that she'd been an author—a successful one apparently. She caught sight of a few awards scattered here and there. Bookshelves lined all the walls, crammed full of leather bound books waiting to greet her like old friends. And there were copies of titles she'd written, thirteen in all. Seeing them again made her tingle with excitement.

"Oh, Mog," she sighed as she approached the cat sunning itself on the window sill. As her fingertips touched his fur, the cat yawned and let out a meow as if asking where she'd been so long. "Oh, how I missed you, you lazy cat."

Her exploring hands touched all her books, palm to leather-bound spine, her eyes drinking in familiar authors and titles until she saw one name in particular embossed in gold. She turned to her guardian angel who had swept her across the threshold into her home, and who lingered silently by the door as she reacquainted herself with her library. Finally she had a name to put to his face. "HG," she told him confidently, "thank you for bringing me home."

No hesitation at all as she'd said those words, it was as if the old her, before the stroke, had reasserted itself in these familiar surroundings and she was whole again.

"You're welcome," he replied, also with no hesitation, so she must have been right in selecting his name.

"I want to write again." Her fingers caressed the tip of her laptop lid. "I have so much catching up to do. So much to tell the world of what was happening while I was away. My readers, my fans …"

"They know," he reassured her. "All your social pages have been regularly updated."

All his doing, she had no doubt now. Like the cat being fed and the dog being walked, and the house kept up to date. He'd seen to it all.

"Oh, you're a good and noble friend, HG. What would I be without you?"

He took a small bow at her compliment, which made her smile even wider.

"I must write!" she declared again, frail fingers fumbling with the laptop.

He crossed the room to her and laid his strong hands lightly across hers. "There'll be time for that later. It's your first day back home. Come and explore the house properly first, maybe sit in the garden for a spell. Remember the doctors told you not to rush things."

And he was right, as she felt he had always been right whenever she'd turned to him for advice in the past. But now that she *did* remember him, she wondered in what context? Friend fitted him easily, but was he her lover? Husband perhaps? A friend wouldn't carry her over the threshold, now, would he?

Bob the dog greeted them in the garden. He didn't seem as exuberant as she remembered, almost as if he sensed she needed to be treated with care. The dog stayed by her side as she and HG sat and talked about her past. She had no doubt that prompting her memory was all part of her recuperation, but she was too shy to tell him she couldn't really remember who he was. It might be just enough of a crack in her defence to have them sending her back to hospital, and she wanted to stay at home now, comforted by all her familiar things. His name had already returned to her. She was sure given time she would remember who he was.

No shy bride on her wedding night, she showed no embarrassment as he helped her bathe and dress for bed. He'd performed these tasks for her in the hospital as well while she'd been recovering, so she was quite comfortable naked in his presence now, and happy to follow his lead.

But when he tucked the duvet over her, kissed her on the cheek, turned and headed for the door she called after him.

"This isn't right, is it? I distinctly recall us sleeping together."

He turned back to her, smiling a little sheepishly. "I thought after your time in hospital you might prefer to sleep alone?"

She patted the duvet beside her decisively and stared him into compliance. He dutifully removed his robe and slippers and slid into bed beside her, enfolding her in his arms.

"Can you hear them too?" she asked him, her head pressed against his chest. He made a noise like a question mark. "My army of nanos, I'm sure I can hear them sweeping their way through my veins making sure I stay alive." He drew her a little closer to him and she was soon asleep and dreaming of angels.

"Welcome home, Miss B," said the lady with the olive complexion and the lovely smile.

Mina ...? Nina ...? Nona! Her cook and housekeeper, who had been with her for ... oh, well over a decade now and was in her middle 40s.

"What will you be having for breakfast? Scrambled eggs? Toast? I can fix you up some waffles if you want?"

Nona had two grown children, three if you counted Grace whom she doted on, tempting her with breakfast treats.

"Oh, waffles I think," Grace said decisively.

A frown shadowed HG's face. "Perhaps the scrambled eggs would be easier for you to eat?" he suggested.

But she made a face. They'd fed her scrambled eggs in the hospital. Horrible stuff made from powdered eggs, reconstituted with water. And she'd eaten it gladly at first, despite it being tasteless, because she'd needed sustenance and it had been easy to swallow. But now that her taste had returned and she was home, Nona's fine waffles beckoned.

"Waffles," she repeated, and Nona smiled at her again and that was the end of that.

But Grace couldn't help noticing the cold face Nona presented to HG. "And will you be breakfasting too, sir?" she asked him.

He seemed to shrink back from the cook's question as if she'd attacked him. Certainly not comfortable in *her* presence. Had they always been at loggerheads, Grace wondered, or was it just that he'd suggested she have something else for breakfast? She tried to search her memories, but nothing came. They'd be worth watching, these two.

Though still a challenge to eat—HG had to help her cut them up into bite-sized pieces—the waffles were divine, and after she'd eaten them old habits rose like ghosts from her mind. "And now I'll go to my office, I think. Check my e-mails, review my notes."

Nona smiled warmly and said, "Just as it's always been," as she cleared away their plates. But Grace saw the dagger-like look she threw at HG, who was also aware of it—Grace had no doubt— but did his best to keep his face neutral. Instead he followed her in to her study like a faithful dog, sitting quietly in the chair in the corner where she recalled Bob liked to lay. His dog then?

No! No, most definitely *her* dog, and usually sitting in the space HG occupied.

He saw her confusion.

"My dog usually sits there. Where is he?"

"In the back yard. Would you like me to bring him in?"

And Bob headed straight for his usual spot in the study, but HG looked around awkwardly for somewhere to sit, and seemed suddenly out of place.

"As I recall," she stated boldly, the laptop finally open before her, "you have your own office further down the house where you write *your* books … when you're not doing something in the garden, that is. You're very good at gardening."

For a moment he looked at her as if their roles were reversed—like *he* had holes in his memory and she knew all his past.

"Today—well, for a while—I think I'd like to stay here with you, watch you work. In case you need me—in case you need to be reminded of anything."

She smiled at him over the laptop screen. He was very kind.

HG settled on the wide windowsill. In time the cat strolled into the study, leapt onto the sill beside him and settled there. Grace got on with her writing.

After a few paragraphs, she beckoned HG over to her laptop. "Does this look right to you?"

He leaned over her shoulder and studied her words, looking for spelling errors, checking that sentences were in order and not scrambled as they'd been in her earlier efforts to write in the hospital. "It looks fine."

"But is it still me, HG? Is it still my voice?"

He frowned, understood her frustrations, reread her words. Of course he'd read all her previous works. Finally he said supportively, "Yes, I think it sounds like you."

She sighed in relief and leaned back against him. "Thank you! I knew I could trust you!" Her withered hand, thin as a bird's foot, reached up to clutch his, and he pulled it to his lips and kissed the fingers from which her livelihood sprang.

"You're welcome, my dear." With that he returned to the wide windowsill with the cat.

Nona arrived bearing a tray laden with a teapot, cup, saucer, sugar bowl, milk jug, all in the Royal Albert design. A plate of scones had also been squeezed onto the tray.

"Time for a break, Miss B," she announced with a smile, but greeted HG with a hostile raised eyebrow which Grace missed.

"Why only one cup, Nona?" Grace queried innocently.

"I thought the … gentleman … was in the garden. "

"A natural oversight," HG spoke up.

"You'll take tea with me, HG?" Grace asked.

"Of course."

Her displeasure conveyed by cold silence, Nona fetched another cup and saucer.

"There you are, Mister…?"

"HG. Just HG."

Grace showed no sign of noticing this inconsistency.

"Mr Peters and Mr Carter said they might visit you later today, Miss B," Nona informed her.

Grace looked up idly from the scone she was carefully spreading with homemade jam. There was a vague expression across her face that suggested she had no idea who these two visitors were.

"Your editor, Mr Peters, and as I recall Mr Carter works in the publicity office of your publishers," HG stepped in to fill the void.

"Oh," Grace said nonplussed, returning her attention to her scone.

"Perhaps when you meet them again …?" HG suggested.

"Perhaps," Grace responded, head down, not wanting to engage, pretending instead to concentrate on her tea. Too many people, too many names to remember, too many thoughts best left in the past. Her brain, once as swift as a greyhound in flight, struggled like a sack full of drowning puppies.

There was a knock on the front door perhaps an hour after they'd had morning tea.

HG was quick to scoot off the wide windowsill, murmuring, "I'll get it."

There was awkward small talk in the hallway, then the two guests were ushered into her office.

Old memories stirred like a cat stretching before a fire on a cold winter's day. The one on the left was Mr Peters. Robert, wasn't it? Robbie? Their exchanges had been light, informal, flirtatious. He'd always tried to jolly her along, even when he brought the worst of news. But that other one ... Carter ... always an ill wind, that one, and from his grave face nothing had changed there.

"You're looking well, Grace." Robbie leaned forward and gave her a peck on the cheek.

"And back to writing already," Carter noted approvingly.

I never liked you, Grace thought. And somehow she found that memory soothing. The man only knew how to communicate in sales figures, print runs and deadlines. He found no joy in the beauty of the written word the way she and Robbie did.

"Another best seller, I hope?" Carter probed.

"I've written 'fish' repeatedly on four pages so far; do you think that will sell?" Grace asked him caustically, enjoying the look of horror that flitted across his face. Even Robbie looked askance as he ducked behind her antique desk to check the small screen of her laptop.

"No she hasn't," he reassured Carter.

"No, it says 'The cat ate the fish' repeatedly for four pages, doesn't it, Robbie?"

Robbie shot a reassuring glance to Carter. "No it doesn't."

"Will you join us for tea?" HG spoke up.

Grace wondered why the other two men acted so awkwardly in his presence. HG was a best-selling author, after all; why didn't he deserve more of their respect? Fascinated, she continued to watch the interplay, or lack of it. What was going on here?

Carter shot a glance to Robbie.

"This is just a whistle-stop visit, I'm sorry, Grace. But we'll pop in and visit you again soon, I promise." Robbie homed in on her cheek for another kiss. "*Au revoir*, my dear. HG, will you see us out?"

And why the devil did they need HG to show them where her front door was? It hadn't moved since they'd used it to gain entrance to her house.

Grace wished she had enhanced hearing so she could better hear the whispered discussion that went on in the hallway, though she could have sworn she'd heard the phrase "strange bedfellows."

HG returned to his spot on the windowsill. Every now and then Grace called on him for assistance with this word or that as she wrote, but when she started talking to him about one of the characters she'd developed, she saw his face momentarily go blank as if he didn't know how to respond. She waited patiently, expectantly, and in time he gave her an answer she found suitable.

"Thank you, HG," she said, finally bringing to a close the conversation that he'd found so challenging.

Nona served them lunch in the back garden, and after lunch, at HG's suggestion, Grace retired to her bed for an afternoon nap. It had been a busy morning, and she still tired easily.

"Stay!" she called as he tried to leave her to her rest. She feebly tapped the bedspread beside her, and he lay there, settling her into his arms. She pressed her head to his chest and observed, "I can hear them again."

"Hear what, my love?" HG asked, puzzled.

"My nano army sweeping away through my veins." She could feel him smile as HG drew her closer.

"Keeping you alive, my love. So you can write more beautiful words." And HG was aware of the smile that played on her lips as she drifted off to sleep.

As the days passed and Grace's confidence in her writing grew, HG removed himself from her office, leaving the windowsill entirely at the cat's disposal, and took to spending more time in his office, where Grace presumed he was also writing.

He was so absorbed in the book he was reading on his laptop that he didn't hear her approach his sanctuary. Something made him glance up towards the door, and there he found her, leaning against the frame, studying him intently.

For a split second he thought she'd finally begun to puzzle over why he was so much younger than her, though from what she said, it was obvious she thought of them as about the same age. Then a split second later he thought she'd worked it all out and he quickly closed the computer screen. He'd observed her brain was mostly lightning quick. She only missed the things she chose to miss.

"What is it, my love?" he asked her, an enquiring smile about his lips.

"You weren't writing?"

"I was revising something I'd written earlier," he said, belatedly realizing the trap he'd set for himself. Hoping she wouldn't ask to view his words.

"Do you think you could come and revise mine?" she asked him.

"Your muse has left you?" he asked her with a raised eyebrow.

"My muse is sitting in his office down the hallway, and I have a horrible bout of writer's block today."

Couldn't be too bad if she was flirtatious, he considered, rising from his seat to accompany her to her den.

He glanced at the screen, instantly realised it was her latest novel, and that she'd added another five thousand words to it since this morning. She was throwing herself at it like a mountain goat at a hill, and not for the first time he wondered if he should counsel her to take her time. But those two from her publishing house always insisted that hard work would do her good.

"You remember how the protagonist was trapped in that cave ...?"

"Tom Burrows, your adventure-seeking librarian, yes?"

"I'm damned if I know how to get him out now."

"Let me see," he said, leaning in over her left shoulder to get a closer look at what was on the screen. "You don't say if he's carrying a length of rope or not. If you mention it in the previous page ...?"

"Rope's a bit passé, isn't it? Besides, it's a subterranean cave."

"With a river running through it perhaps?"

She considered that for a moment then dismissed it. "How about he feels a breeze on his cheek and follows it to another exit?" she suggested, inspired by his closeness.

He considered this a moment and said, "Yes, that would do it too, I guess."

"Thank you, HG, you're a treasure." She resumed typing, her bird claw-like hands fluttering over the keyboard.

"Why don't you take a break?" he suggested.

She hummed him away dismissively, fingers still flying as she tried to capture words and lodge them on the screen.

He persisted. "Then why not use the speak function on the computer?"

"You know how I hate to use that, HG. It interrupts the flow of the movie in my mind." The words didn't stop spilling onto the screen as she answered him, he noticed.

"Leave you in peace, shall I?" he suggested and she hummed him away.

Back in his office, HG decided it might be wise, considering he was supposed to be a writer, if he had some of his writing to show her just in case she asked to see his work next time she was standing at his door with writers' block. *But what to write?*

He pondered, he played, but noticed the words did not escape from his fingers to the keyboard with the same velocity as they did when she had mastery over them. And they didn't sing as sweetly when they were all aligned like hers did. He frowned at the screen. There turned out to be a lot more to writing than there appeared, but he stuck with it long into the night until she was standing at his office doorway once again, looking peeved.

"HG?"

Something registered in him that this wasn't the first time she'd called his name.

"You didn't come out for dinner," she said, just a hint of irritation in her voice.

"Not hungry," he said dismissively, eyes never leaving the screen. He thought he was on the verge of cracking the code. It had taken him all afternoon, but he thought he was shaping into a reasonably proficient writer.

"Just as well. Nona's long gone, though I could make you a sandwich or something?" she offered with a small smile. He glanced up to acknowledge her and shook his head to her offer, then his attention returned to his work. "Not tired either, I bet? Well, I'm off to bed."

He knew that was a hint for him to escort her to bed, lay down beside her, let her rest her head on his chest. He went to close his program, had a second thought, had a third to dismiss the second, turned it off and followed her to bed, even though he yearned to stay and play with the words some more. It was addictive, this writing she did.

"Maybe you'll let me read it tomorrow?" she asked as she settled in the bed next to him. Her suggestion filled him with delight for reasons that he couldn't fathom.

The anxiety HG felt as Grace sat at his computer reading his words was alien to him. He was surprised at how he waited pensively for her verdict on what he'd written.

"Not bad," she finally said, passing judgement on his words.

The thrill he felt at her approval was completely unexpected.

"It needs a little tightening here, and here, I think," she said, pointing. "And what made you go back to short stories all of a sudden? You haven't written one of those in years."

"Seeing you in hospital," he answered. "Realising none of us are sure of how long we have." Then hesitantly he added: "Do you think it's publishable?"

"Definitely. It just needs a little work, then I suggest you e-mail it to Colin for that magazine he puts out. They'd be proud to have a story from you grace their pages. Now will you help me with my book? I've hit a hard spot again."

HG complied, surreptitiously asking her the name of Colin's magazine before returning to his work. He made good use of her suggestions on how to improve his story and quietly e-mailed it away at the end of the day, saying in his covering letter that Grace had suggested he submit it to them, not sure of what to expect.

"They accepted my story!" HG crowed to Grace, who seemed unfazed by the news that thrilled him. "Well, of course they did," she replied as if she hadn't expected anything else. "You're a good writer and it's a good story."

Grace was so engrossed in her writing that she didn't register the ring of the doorbell, or that Peters and Carter were in the hallway outside having a heated discussion in whispers with HG until several comments had been said above a whisper. Carter hissed something about "This isn't what you were engaged for." At least that's what Grace thought he said, as she headed out to the hall to see what all the fuss was about. The talk lapsed into silence the second she arrived, a sure sign that what they were all talking about concerned her.

"What's the problem here?" she enquired when the silence stretched between the argumentative men gathered in her hallway. And they all looked guilty, which put her more on her guard.

"My bank account ... isn't recognized," HG answered her. He seemed crest-fallen over something.

Carter seemed to rail at that remark. "It's been deleted," he said through gritted teeth.

"I can't get paid for that story I've sold."

Grace frowned. "Get them to pay me, and I'll give HG the money. You'd better sort it out with the bank immediately, HG. And your PayNow account? That hasn't been breached, has it?"

He raised an eyebrow of understanding. "I'll have to check."

He made his way to his office down the hall as Carter and Peters were ushered into Grace's inner sanctum to review the nearly completed manuscript that suddenly she had doubts about. Fear clutched her heart with icy fingers.

They read, they approved, they left. Carter in particular had the happy glint of bestseller profits in his eyes as he departed, but Grace still had her doubts. She summoned HG from his office urgently.

"What is it, my love?" He could see her uncertainty, the worried look on her face.

"Read this manuscript out loud for me, HG, from this page here."

She'd only written those words this afternoon. They were fresh, he hadn't looked at them yet, couldn't extrapolate the new words from what she'd written so far, if her greatest fears were based in truth.

And he read them back to her, word perfect, raising a quizzical eyebrow to her when he'd finished. The confidence with which she had greeted the threesome in the hallway was nowhere to be seen.

"Yes ... that sounds like me. That *is* what's written there, isn't it, HG?"

"Of *course*, my love." His answer emphatic.

"Prove it to me. Type in a line or two and let me read them back to you."

And he did, and she was relieved to find that she could read them back to him in the order he had written them, not like when she was in hospital. But HG still didn't understand what was tormenting her so.

There was quiet desperation in her eyes and on her face as she grasped his arm and said, "You'd tell me the truth, wouldn't you, HG? If this was all an elaborate mock up and my brain was too addled to write any more?"

And now he understood the cause of her anxiety. "I'd tell you, dearest. But would that buffoon, Carter, be hovering around you, urging you to complete your book if he couldn't sell it?"

She conceded him the point, the anxiety fading from her face.

HG had been informed that this flip from confidence to self-doubt was a residue of the stroke, and this wasn't the first manifestation of it. Grace had been working herself so hard lately, as if she hadn't been seriously ill and could continue writing at her old cracking pace. He should have been paying closer attention, anticipating her need for breaks away from the writing that obsessed and frustrated her.

"I tell you what, why don't you take the afternoon off? We could take Bob down to the beach for a walk."

"I'm not sure I could walk that far and back anymore."

"Then we'll take the car. Let the salt air clear your mind, get the feel of sand between your toes. Watch that damned dog of yours leap half way up the sky trying to catch seagulls. You'll feel better for it, I promise you."

And as Bob ran along the beach before them and leaped half way up the sky chasing seagulls who laughed in squawks as they escaped him, Grace gave voice to all her fears. "How much sand is left in my hourglass, do you suppose?" She bent and grabbed a fistful of sand which now slipped through her fingers and blew away to demonstrate. Before HG could formulate an answer she continued, "Do you know, when I first saw you in the hospital, I thought you were an angel sent to carry me to the other side? I was sure I was dying, that my time had run out."

"They managed to bring you back," he told her quietly. "And when they inserted your nanos—well they filled the hourglass to the brim again, so you have all the time in the world. No need to push yourself so hard, my dearest."

"But I feel I'm running out of time. I have so many books I need to write …"

"And you will, my love, you will," he tried to soothe her. "And I will help you in any way I can."

He suggested they lay down together when they got back home, and he checked her health while she slept. The nanos were working perfectly, she seemed well in all other regards too, though she felt a little lighter as she pressed against him. He hadn't been monitoring all her meals—Nona was still hostile towards him—but he was sure she got enough sleep. Every night her head rested on his chest and she slept deeply while he did research and thought up story ideas of his own. She seemed a little fatigued, but that was a lasting after-effect of the stroke from what he'd been told. And this necessity to write, this compulsion that burned in her with a fever pitch, well, that could have something to do with the stroke as well. Couldn't it? He'd have to investigate further, but he thought he was coming to understand what drove her.

It seemed he'd been bitten by the same bug. He'd submitted another short story, and was working on another six stories on his computer while she worked in her office every day. He thought he'd try his hand at a novel soon, he was feeling that good about his emerging skills. And she'd sorted out an online bank account for him. Even though it was linked to her accounts, he could draw on it whenever he felt the need, and it still held the payment he'd received for his first story.

It wasn't supposed to happen like this. He knew it, Carter and Peters knew it, Nona knew it, and in her own way, he expected even Grace knew it, despite the clever web of deception she wove around herself to make him appear a natural part of her life. It was because she needed him. Though to anyone who didn't know her, she still appeared fiercely independent, she made room for him not only in her life but in her past, so that they could have a future together.

"There, I think it's finally done," Grace said, her hands raising off the computer keyboard with a pianist's flourish.

They were words HG thought he'd never hear. She'd been revising her manuscript, making minor corrections for the past six weeks, and while Robbie had been encouraging whenever he visited, or read her work in progress, HG had come to see why she'd resented Carter so much. He'd done nothing but nag her to finish the manuscript, and HG's efforts to protect her had seen him receive a tongue lashing for having his own developing career. It wasn't why he'd been engaged. It wasn't right. It wasn't done.

And the man was adamant that Grace should do a promotional tour when the book came out. HG wasn't so sure about that. While meeting her fans would boost her spirits—he didn't doubt it for a second—he worried that it would exhaust her. Carter seemed to think she was capable of the same pounding schedule she'd kept before her stroke, but nanos or not, she was a more fragile creature these days. Everything she had was channelled into keeping that little flame of creativity alive and burning in her.

There was not an awful lot left for anything else, though she always seemed to have time for him.

When it came to the tour, HG found an unexpected ally in Robbie. They were able to cut down the number of appearances Grace was to make, and argue for longer breaks at home before she did another leg of the tour. Robbie and HG would also be joined by several more minders on tour, despite Carter huffing and puffing about the extra cost. She was worth it, Robbie reminded him sharply. She'd been their top-selling author for years now, and he wanted her to hold that position for years to come.

"I feel like a broken down old racehorse," Grace said as the men all argued around her as if she couldn't hear them, couldn't speak her own mind. "Will she make it through one more campaign? Or should we cut our losses and send her to the glue factory now?"

While the two from the publishers traded verbal blows, HG homed in on her voice, caught her hand up in his and kissed her fingers. "Put out to stud perhaps," he suggested, and it made her laugh the way he'd hoped it would.

"I'm too old for that as well! I'll be fine with you beside me, HG. And if not you, then Robbie when you feel you need a break. You'll both look after me, I'm sure."

And they did, Robbie and HG took it in turns to sit beside her as she signed her books for delighted fans overjoyed to see her recovered from her stroke and creating again. Many brought her flowers, chocolates, gifts, which she received like a queen, thanking the givers before handing their presents on to HG or Robbie, whoever was closest, to store away until later.

In one instance, as she passed him a small posy of flowers she'd been given, Grace called HG by name. As he took the posy, the present-giver in front of Grace reached out a tentative hand and lightly brushed his fingers. "I like your work too," she told him shyly, and he was as surprised by her words as how they made him feel.

Grace watched his reaction to the compliment and chuckled throatily. "Why, HG, I believe you're blushing!"

At night in strange hotel rooms, when she could no longer type the words for her next novel into her laptop, she'd lay on the bed and dictate, and HG would dutifully transcribe her words into the machine. And when her words slowed and stopped because she had finally drifted off to sleep, he kept writing.

She noticed. He knew she would because he realised by now that writing fiction was like having babies; you instantly recognized what was yours. Sometimes he'd see her smile as she revised her work and found his words entwined with hers like lovers wrapped about each other celebrating spring. She delighted at the union of their words, themselves.

"I don't have much time left," she'd whisper to him.

"You can't know that." He'd try to jolly her out of her paranoia with a half-smile, but she obsessed about it.

"I know," she stated with a fierceness that frightened him.

Grace, who had prowled the world like a solitary lioness in her prime, looked at him with the shining eyes of a huntress; yet he was not her prey, and she would not devour him. They would hunt words down together for as long as she had left.

*

"The tour is exhausting her," HG reported to Robbie privately, knowing he could rely on Robbie's sympathy. "She needs rest, and a new infusion of nanites—"

"The doctors gave us a ten year guarantee," Robbie interrupted, surprised.

"Her body continues to deteriorate. You're all expecting too much of her; she expects too much of herself, and she's pushing herself too hard. I fear she's heading for another stroke."

"But the nanites are there to stop that."

"They can't make her immortal. If her body deteriorates faster than they can repair it, if she has a bad fall, if her heart stops beating while she sleeps ..."

"Then it's your job to restart it, isn't it? What do you think we got you for? We've invested a lot of money in her, we expect to recoup it."

HG observed how similar Robbie sounded to Carter, but kept his thoughts to himself. "She has given her all to her writing, to you as her publishers, to her fans ... but sooner or later ..." The death sentence hung between them. "She needs time to rest, regain her strength."

And yet HG, more than anyone, knew whatever drove her raged hotter than what fuelled him. She was like a dying star, and yet she seemed intent on hurtling towards oblivion as fast as she could, with not a minute's care for the world she'd leave behind, or the sorrow her passing would cause.

But how could she know? Why was she so sure she was dying when no test he could run on her could confirm it?

She was looking so weak and tired, her skin pale, splotched and brittle like old paper, that they ended her tour early. She didn't even fight their decision. In more than one way she leaned against HG for strength, and with all the nobility she could muster, she acquiesced to his pushing her around in a wheel-chair. Like night after sunset, her end was drawing in.

One night as they lay together in her big bed, her head resting on his chest listening to the wheels and cogs of his heart, she said, "You don't know how much it pains me to tell you this, HG, but I fear I must leave you soon."

And as she spoke the words he heard his mechanical heart break. How could she know? No human he encountered came with an expiry date tattooed on their body. Yet he accepted that somehow she knew more than he did.

"My love," he murmured, and he squeezed her bird-like hand in his, felt her flutter beside him.

"Now you mustn't worry, HG. You'll be taken care of. I've seen to it. What's mine is yours and always has been."

"And what's mine is yours, and forever will be." He kissed her lightly on the forehead as tears formed in his eyes.

He listened to her through the night as she slept, listened to the silence when she'd drawn her last rattling breath and her heart stopped beating. For a time the nanites whirred around her, trying to make her heart beat again, push the blood through her veins. He could almost taste their confusion and sadness. They had failed. In time they too succumbed to silence. And he didn't stir until dawn, even though the protocol was programmed into him to keep her alive no matter what the cost. He over-rode it. She had worked hard enough for those who would exploit her. It was time to let her go.

When Nona called her down for breakfast, HG carefully disengaged himself from her cold, still, body, tried to gather his courage, his thoughts. He had played through this scene all through his lonely night. He hadn't anticipated Nona's scream when he told her, though. While there'd always been distance between them, now she looked at him as if he were a monster.

She raced up the stairs to see for herself, and her wailing for Grace filled the house. She was inconsolable, so it fell to him to call Robbie and Carter to let them know.

At least their responses were predictable. Carter flew into a fine rage. "Back in your box!" he yelled at HG, no need to even play at civility now that Grace was gone. "Our contract with you is terminated."

HG nodded acquiescence of his situation, and merely held out a sheet of paper for Carter to read.

Carter naturally expected it to be the contract, but was surprised to find he was looking at a page from a story.

"Grace's work, undoubtedly" he proclaimed, having read it. "Did she finish a final novel and secrete it away from us by any chance?"

Astute as ever, HG saw the dollar signs illuminate Carter's eyes. "Grace's and *my* work. Can you tell who wrote which line ...?" His eyebrow arched as if to say, "What was that about getting into a box?"

"But you *can't!*" Carter all but exploded. "You're a *machine!*" That last word was spat out of his mouth as if it were the vilest of insults.

HG cocked his head in acknowledgement. "Indeed. But one that's learned to write fiction in his own voice, as well as imitate hers."

Carter blustered before him. "You've experienced a little success, I grant you, but only through your association with her. Your efforts are that of an awkward beginner—"

"Pinpoint my words on that page then, if they are so crass."

Carter read the page again, and couldn't differentiate.

"A trick," he declared indignantly. "You've merely printed out a page of Grace's writing and you're trying to trick me."

"And why would I do that, Mr Carter?"

"So we don't decommission you."

"I think you'll find it hard to decommission me when you read her will. I am the sole beneficiary of her estate."

"But you're a mechanoid! You can't inherit, you aren't a legal entity."

"I was real enough for Grace. And, of course, you're well within your rights to contest her will through the courts—but think of the publicity it will generate."

"That could well go against us," Robbie supplied, picturing the global news headlines once the word got out.

"Whereas, if you were agreeable, I could go on to complete Grace's latest novel … perhaps even write several more."

Carter examined the paper in his hands again.

"We can't keep her death from her public."

"Nor should we. But it wouldn't be anything unusual to find early drafts of unfinished works when clearing up her estate, now would it?"

Carter looked stunned, but HG knew he had won. He'd live on because of Grace, and she'd live on because of him.

I think 'HG' owes part of its existence to my watching the early days of my father's recovery from a stroke. I was fascinated with how his injured mind found detours around the mental road-blocks as he learned to communicate again. He knew he drove an "Oh, what a feeling!" for instance, but couldn't think of "Toyota" until prompted.

'HG' was published in Andromeda Spaceways Inflight Magazine *Issue 54. Editor: Simon Petrie.*

All But A Few

All but a few of us
Are left behind now.

When he talked to her,
She could not believe,
Such a handsome form
Could come to one like she.
That human girl,
That normal girl,
He had taken up with.

When he touched her,
He could not see,
The pleasure quiver of her skin,
When touched by alien hand,
In open places,
Where few have right to be sensitive.

And when she rubbed her head on his shoulder,
As once she'd done,
When she'd had a horn,
He thought it just expressive mimicry.

And when she tossed her head,
In the sunlight,
He was too earth-blind,
To see the rainbows form.

Oh, but when she ran towards him that day,
A straight-out charge,
To greet the dawn,
He saw it then,
Her noble horn,
The now-white coat, the tassled beard.
He saw her then,
A Unicorn.
And knew she'd been that all along.

Published in Starkindler *No 7 (circa 1984)*

Off Course Of Course

Any mother who's ever had a child that has been left out from a kids' gang, or game, will know that confused, hurt look of being excluded, made to feel inferior.

He's not my child. He's not even my unicorn, but we hang around together.

I want to be a writer. He wants to be a racehorse. Maybe none of us are happy with what we truly are.

On moonlit nights when no-one's looking, he likes to wander up to the racecourse, not three blocks from where we live, hurl himself past the post and pretend he's winning the Melbourne Cup.

Even unicorns have their fantasies.

In the hushed pre-dawn of early morning I hear him clatter up the side passage that runs along our house. I know just where he's going as I roll over and go back to sleep. He's hobnobbing with the thoroughbreds. Or trying to. They're snobby horses who like to spurn him.

Don't they know that unicorns are synonymous with perfection?

And then he comes back, looking dejected because they wouldn't let him play with them again.

Like me and my writing, I try to console him that not everybody has to like you, they don't always see you for what you really are, but you have to keep on pounding away.

Things must be getting a little better up at the race track though. The thoroughbreds must be accepting him just a little, even if they aren't all falling over themselves to be his friend, his stablemate.

He's been coming home from the racecourse looking not quite so distraught of late. Seeming content, even pleased with himself, he'll nuzzle me with his velvet muzzle and whisper the latest racing tips in my ear.

Published in Antipodean SF, issue 18, 1999. Editor: Ion Newcombe.

'Next!' Cried the Faun

"Next!" cried the faun, emerging from the bushes. His round cheeks were rosy from his exertions with a maiden who'd been left to pull on her clothes and stumble away. He snatched a bunch of grapes from a nearby silver serving dish and stuffed them into his mouth, painting his cheeks and lips purple with grape juice. How he loved the rites of spring!

Three girls in diaphanous gowns all looked shyly from one to another, then at him as they giggled behind their hands. Which of them would go next?

Hanging further back from this group, Petra punched Helen in the small of her back, impatient with her dowdy friend looking out of place and awkward in her summer shift and crown of flowers.

"Well go on then, what are you waiting for? Two springs have passed since you came of age, and you haven't offered your flower to anyone yet. Now, I've filled you with wine and honeycakes, you should be nice and relaxed. Just get it over with, will you? I have a date with a faun myself this afternoon." She winked lasciviously to Helen who seemed stunned by this disclosure.

"You do it more than once?" Helen looked askance.

"Of course. It's fun."

"But I thought it was only the first time …"

"I bet you thought if you did it once you could go back to your books, your painting and your tapestries, and put it all behind you? Honestly, Helen, what is wrong with you?"

But Helen was again distracted by the intercourse between the three maidens and the faun. The girls, it seemed, had decided who would be next, and two of them pushed the third towards the faun. They all giggled. The goat boy's little tail waggled with anticipation as he took the maiden deep within his lair among the bushes.

As with all the others Helen had observed, there came the girl's sharp cry of pain, followed by placating words from the faun, and then more moaning from the girl that Helen had to admit didn't sound anything like an expression of pain.

"See? Nothing to it! Just a little prick at first ..." Petra broke into giggles at her own joke, while Helen stared at her, uncomprehending.

The bushes that hid the faun's lair shook violently with the inhabitants' passion as both moaned in unison. The maid called out urgently, "Yes! Yes! Deeper! Oh!!!" The faun gave a few grunts and something that sounded like a bleat then the maiden cried, "Oh!" again, but it seemed to have the ring of disappointment about it, as if to say: *Is that all I get? Is there no more?*

They heard the slap of a hand on a round, ripe buttock, which appeared to be the faun's signal that the entanglement was over. "Put your clothes back on, there's a good girl. I might see you again sometime. NEXT!"

"Go *on*!" Petra enthused, pushing at Helen's shoulder. She'd promised Helen's father that *this* year it would be done. Then he could marry Helen off without any problems. She'd know what to expect in the bed chamber on her wedding night.

But the more Helen observed, the less inclined she was to participate in the deflowering ceremony as part of the rites of spring.

All she wanted was the peace and quiet she found amongst her books and needlework. The love of learning, she was sure, would provide all the passion she would ever need.

"He's looking this way." Petra grabbed Helen by the arm, intent on dragging her to the faun if she must.

Feeling trapped, Helen panicked. She shook herself from Petra's grasp. "No, I can't! I just can't!" She pulled free, running away from the meadow with all its smells and sounds of springtime rutting.

It wasn't that she was averse to coupling with a male faun *per se*, it was just that it all seemed so … debauched, lacking in decorum … in emotional engagement. There had to be a better way, surely? A meeting of souls, a union of minds?

When she'd tried to explain these things to Petra, her friend had rolled her eyes, telling Helen not to believe everything she read in her books. Real life was not like that at all, and Helen needed to get out and live a little.

But Helen lived plenty, in her books. Words that lifted her spirit on the wings of doves or eagles, and opened her eyes to other worlds. That was bliss for her … not this carnal grubbing in the dirt that seemed to excite Petra so much.

Petra's voice calling her to come back was soon far behind her. Though awkward and ungainly, Helen could be fleet of foot when the need took her. Chances were, Petra would take the wrong path, or give up and return to the fauns in the glade before finding her, but she ran on through the woods just in case.

A stitch in her side finally forced her to stop. She glanced behind her, making sure she'd recognise the path back should she need to use it, but she wasn't feeling lost.

She noticed the luscious scent of jasmine at the same moment the sound of pipes wafting on the breeze caressed her ears.

A haunting, lilting lament that hinted of love lost and sadness. Carefully, she made her way through the woods, following the music until she came upon a clearing.

He sat on a rock outcropping, naked back turned to the hot midday sun, all his concentration on the twin pipes—notoriously difficult to play—his breathing, fingering, and the notes that he created. A musician at one with the moment.

Another goat boy! Helen thought in disgust. The woods were teeming with them this time of year. Yet this one seemed older, more mature. His beard was fully formed, not the tufts of fluff of the ardent stud she'd left behind. And he had a serious demeanour—at least while he was engaged in his music. She was sure he had no idea that she was his audience of one, feeling his music tug at her soul. And because he was unaware of her, she stilled, relaxed, let down her guard and gave in to the haunting melody that he made.

When he released the final notes of his song, looking up at the sky as if watching his music fly free, and a silent stillness descended on the glade, Helen felt compelled to applaud his performance. He was startled to discover her sharing his sheltered space and his innermost thoughts.

"Who are you?" he inquired, turning pale grey eyes to regard her intently as if she were some oddity.

"Helen," she responded, feeling very self-conscious. An intruder here. "I followed the music," she said by way of apology. "You play beautifully." She was aware that she was babbling meaningless platitudes, and he looked away as if he knew that was all they were as well.

Then coyly he looked back, wanting more of her honey-dipped words.

"Where did you learn to play?" She struggled to say something that would hold his interest.

"I was taught when I was very young," he replied curtly, his eyes drifting away as boredom threatened to replace coyness.

"Do you read at all?" She offered kindling to keep the spark of conversation burning between them, and was nearly burned by the flame of passion in his eyes.

"I have an extensive library! Would you like to see it? I have spiced wine, or could offer you tea if you prefer? And I baked a fresh batch of oatcakes just this morning." His hooves caused sparks to fly as he scampered off his rock outcropping, offering his hand to her, and indicating his little house.

"But I don't even know your name," she said, shyly slipping her hand into his.

"Fox," he answered her. And as an explanation, the sun highlighted the copper red in his hair.

"Sly then?" she asked him.

"Wise," he replied, as he led her across the threshold.

"This is my library." He guided her to a wall full of shelves all stacked with tomes, leatherbound, musky smelling, well loved, well thumbed. A king's ransom of knowledge. "What is it you would like to drink?"

They stared again into each other's eyes, a little too deeply, a little too longingly.

"You." If she hadn't said it with her mouth, her body had shouted it, and all pretence of hospitality dropped away from him, just as any pretence of unwillingness dropped away from her, soon to be followed by her dress and garland of flowers. Their lips met, then set out like explorers conquering new worlds. They touched at first, then smelled and licked each other, fingers acting as cartographers, mapping the new body each explored.

They struggled to contain their burning desire for each other as they awkwardly made their way to his bed—wide enough for two, the bedding smelling of goat, but at least it was private here, no blue sky above them, or others listening in the wings; not like rutting in a hedge. Was it … dignified? Helen considered, but the scent of his musk infiltrated her nostrils and inflamed her passion, and she knew that, if not dignified, at least it was right.

"Please, this is—I mean I haven't …" she tried to warn him as their petting grew more intimate.

He stopped sucking her breast for a moment to look up at her and ask, "For you too?"

His raised eyebrow was matched by hers. Each had thought the other was well versed in the ways of love. Now they paused, reconsidered. "We'll learn together then," Fox announced, and that settled it.

His tongue, that so artfully brought forth exquisite music from his pipes, touched her in her most private places and compelled her to cry out pretty notes of her own. In his turn, he discovered she possessed a talented pair of lips, and could play him delightfully.

They tossed and tumbled, cried and moaned, shrieked and shouted, and when it was all over, when they were laying panting speechless on sweaty sheets, they both laughed at the intensity of the ecstasy they had managed to generate in each other.

"I believe I was going to offer you a drink," Fox said finally, when the power of speech had returned to him.

"Yes, I believe you were." Helena looked at him with sanguine eyes. "And introduce me to your library."

Fox struggled from his bed to reluctantly pursue his role of gentleman host. "Spiced wine?"

"Would be lovely. Thank you," Helen answered as she plucked her dress from the floor and covered herself.

Each with a goblet of fragrant wine, they stood side by side, not touching, as Fox showed Helen the treasures in his library. His collection was diverse: books on gardening, philosophy, music and poetry, as well as parchments with music and poems he had written himself. He wanted her to be impressed by his collection of knowledge, creative talents and refined tastes, and she was, but as he concluded his tour of his treasured library, Helen was nudging him towards his bed again … there was another subject she wanted to explore.

Not quite able to believe his luck, Fox followed Helen to the bed again and they rediscovered the journey they had earlier taken together.

Sated, they reclined amongst his tousled bedclothes, still trying to catch their breath.

"You're fantastic!" Helen said. "I didn't know it could be like this."

Fox giggled delightedly. "Neither did I." He wasn't sure of how to fill the silence that followed. Finally he said, "Would you like me to play you one of my own compositions on my pipes?"

"That would be delightful," Helen agreed.

Fox fetched his pipes and a piece of parchment, and played to her. Her eyes drifted closed and a smile graced her lips. She let his music carry her away, but her thoughts kept drifting back to this new subject she'd discovered. Though not like her books and tapestries, still she wanted to pursue love with the same passion she'd applied to acquiring other forms of knowledge. When his song was finished, she looked at him with eyes that spoke of her endless hunger to learn more.

The intensity of her gaze made him nervous, like living next to a volcano. She was hot and smouldering.

He so wanted to make love to her again, to learn more about her body, about their shared pleasure, But that thought scared him; what if he was like all the other fauns, after all? He had devoted his life to other things—higher, more pure loves. There were still books to read, music to write. And all she wanted to do was—as lovely as that was …

Helen reached for him. He pulled away, asking instead if he could read to her. Clearly, she had an intellect comparable to his, for she was familiar with the great authors whose works he had collected. For a while she was soothed by his reading and, when he suggested it, even read to him. It distracted her for an hour or so, but he could see her passion for him building in every smouldering gaze she sent his way.

"I'm not like the other fauns," he tried to explain, his little tail shaking nervously.

"I know you're not." Hunger dripped from every word.

"I don't want the other fauns," she continued. "I don't think I even want men. From what I've seen of them, they're brainless, insensitive brutes who only know how to drink until they're drunk, mate and fight. But you … you have imagination, education, and an intellect. I want *you*."

He blinked a few times at the intensity of her words. "But there's so much more we have in common. I thought we two wanted to pursue the higher truths—books, music, art."

"I've found the lower truths aren't so bad either," Helen purred.

"Yes, well …" It had been well worth revisiting, but for now, he was satisfied—tired, even—and he wanted time alone so he could compose music in her honour, write poetry to capture what she'd done to his heart. Later, he would play it for her outside in the garden, with her head resting in his lap while the sun shone down, and …

"Helen, what are you doing?" Her look of hunger for him had been replaced by a summer thunderstorm of rage, and he could read the anger in her movement as she put on her dress.

"Make love to your music, your art and your poems then!" she spat as she stalked past him, heading back to the meadow where other fauns were servicing the local maidens. "I'm not waiting for you."

Perplexed, unaware that he was the cause of her mercurial mood swing, he let her walk out of his life, even as he searched for fresh parchment and quill so that he could pen an ode to her.

"Next!" Her voice came back on the breeze to taunt him.

'Next! Cried the Faun' was published in the Next *anthology (CSFG Publishing, 2013). Editors: Simon Petrie and Rob Porteous.*

Everybody Wants To Be St George

If you were to ask me what I know about living, my answer would be: not much for a Lord or a Lady, but plenty for a tavern keeper.

Wine, mead, beer and drunks, I know them well. Wits, philosophical fools and foolish philosophers, I've seen my share of them too. And the down-trodden, and the down-hearted; men who'd slit your throat if you looked at them the wrong way, and women who'd bed anyone for the dregs of their goblets (and plump purses later, I do not doubt it.)

If observing this mass of humanity is life, then yes, I've seen it.

But my friend, Naramat (for I choose to call him my friend), he is truly different. He exists apart from life. And I feel my story with him is worth telling.

Now Naramat was a casual-regular drinker in my tavern. (Which, by the way, is called The Warlock's Rest should you ever wish to quench your thirst and spend your copper, gold or silver there.) I saw him for a few days at a time every now and again. Unlike some of my patrons, there was no fixed time or day when he might visit us. Like smoke, he was unpredictable in his patterns, but whenever he appeared we made him welcome. Sometimes he'd take food and lodgings with us, sometimes he would go elsewhere for his bed and food, and sometimes his stays weren't long enough to warrant accommodation save a chair by the fire to warm his weary bones.

A great one for the comfort of warmth was Naramat.

If you asked me his age, I could give you no accurate answer. For while there was grey nobly tinting his mass of hair and beard (and had been for as long as I had known him), his eyes shone, at times, with the eagerness of youth. And yet at other times he spoke with the knowledge that can only be accumulated over several lifetimes. Truly, his age I know not, and nor should it matter, only that he seemed indifferent to the years and our time.

Yes, our Naramat was different.

Of all the patrons that have drunk at my inn (and in my time I've seen a few) only he could turn my heart away from its love of profit. For a copper coin he could buy a jug of mead; and I would refill it for him all night long if need be, as if he had invested gold for every cup he drank. He did not always pay in copper. On odd occasions he gave me silver, and once he gave me gold. He would share his monetary riches with you if he had them, though like the rest of us mostly he was poor.

What he lacked in terms of the quality or the frequency of his coins, he more than made up for with his presence. It was a pleasure to merely be in his company, and there were many who would stay longer in my tavern, buy more drink, perhaps a meal, when Naramat was there. It was a pure joy for him to look at you with those smiling eyes and talk to you in his voice as warm as any fire and as gentle as a feather's falling touch. Or at least that's how it seemed to me.

Though he wasn't a fast drinker, he was also neither a drunkard, for which I was grateful, because men are most ugly and repulsive when they're most vulnerable from too much drink. You're exposed to their innermost thoughts and emotions as they scream and yell, create havoc in their wake, or cry like babies into their cups.

I remember so well one of Naramat's visits ... There weren't many patrons in the tavern on this particular day, but Naramat was among them, drinking slowly, listening thoughtfully and giving his opinion, or passing the time of day with those who sought him out. As the day progressed, after catching up with those he knew, and sharing in the conversation, he had drifted away to sit by himself.

I watched him playing idly with his goblet, staring at it as if he held the entire world in his hands. I walked up to him, pitcher at the ready.

"Here, Naramat, let me refill that for you."

"Thank you, Amirer," he said, his blue eyes shining at me. "You're very kind to me."

It was not his way to show his thanks by flirting with you the way some of the drinkers will. I liked that about him. You get tired of hearing the same old lies, especially when the speaker thinks he's the originator of the same sad old sayings, no matter how well-meant they're offered.

"You bring us luck, Narramat. I've always told you so."

He flashed me a quick grin. "You bring luck upon yourself," he replied simply.

As things were quiet in the tavern, I sat opposite him. He'd been sitting alone for a while now, and I thought he might want a bit of company. "What troubles you, Naramat? You seem unusually quiet."

"Do I indeed? I'll try my best to cheer myself up for you."

"No, don't try. If you feel melancholy, then that is your entitlement. Don't try to impress me with your laughter if you'd rather be sheltered in your own thoughts. I'd best be about my chores."

I noticed there was another customer waiting patiently at the bar, but as I got up to go serve him, Naramat lightly grabbed my hand.

"How long since you've had a man in your bed? " he asked me, and his question threw me into confusion.

"Long enough so I don't miss the presence, " I answered him with the first thing that came into my head. *Not so long that I've forgotten what it's like*, I thought, but he was no mind-reader. He turned his head to his goblet, and I went off to serve my customer, wondering over what might have been an offer.

There had been a man to share my bed once. I'm glad he died before he had the opportunity to gamble and drink me out of everything I'd worked so long and hard to buy: my tavern. I'd be penniless and sleeping in the streets now if he'd not been banished from this world. I like being a businesswoman who does not earn a living by laying on her back, and I was never one for chasing and marrying the richest man I could find.

I'm not dependent on any one man. Ah, but I'd be destitute if I could not rely on all of those who drank in my tavern a little more frequently than Naramat did!

I was made aware of another presence in my tavern by the front door being left open overly long and the sharp, cold breeze that scouted about the room, seeking out all our hearts, let in like a mongrel dog. I looked up to see a quest-seeking young fool posing in the doorway as if to impress us all. (I for one was unimpressed.) Then someone did the right thing and shouted, "Shut the flamin' door, Squire!"

The young man looked a little flustered as he followed the instruction.

I deduced by his attention-seeking entrance that he was someone who thought (and thought all others should know) that he was on an important quest. His kind are good for business when their pouches are full and their bellies are empty, but do try me sorely when their money bags are empty and their bellies are full with drink fuelling their bravado. As I was unsure of his financial position, I was prepared to let him stay awhile. Or at least I was until he pinpointed Naramat then marched defiantly to stand in front of him and sneer to make his presence known.

"Keeper," I called softly to the strongman I employ to keep the peace for me. With his shaven, shiny head, gypsy earring, menacing gaze and prominent muscles, ofttimes his presence alone was all that was needed to ensure things didn't get out of hand.

The Keeper emerged from the room out the back, behind the bar. I pointed to the sprite who by now had moved from Naramat; he was parading around the room, seeking to entertain other patrons with his boastings. I've seen my share of story-tellers, professional and amateur, come into the bar, but he had a long way to go before he'd be one of them. All his show and bravado didn't quite cut the mustard when he was clearly still wet behind the ears; still, others appeared to listen, to be polite if nothing else. Naramat's attention stayed on his drink, or possibly this was a ruse.

"These are such fine leather breeks, gentlemen! " the young man was boasting. "Completely waterproof, and do any of you know why?"

"Aye, he's right pissed himself and you can't see the wet patch!" One of my regulars cut the young sire a dose of humility.

The others in the room chuckled, but he went on regaling regardless of the put-down. "They're made of dragon skin, sirs. Come feel for yourselves!"

"Well, granted you've got nice eyes, but don't you think we should be introduced first?" another of my regular crowd voiced to even more laughter. They were ripe for some free entertainment at the expense of this young man, and for a moment I was hoping the problem would be solved with laughter, the whelp would slink off back into the cold from whence he came. But no, he was determined to make a loud, showy nuisance of himself regardless.

He crossed back to Naramat. "I need a jerkin and cloak of the same magical substance to complete my outfit," he said pointedly. "But first I need a dragon."

"Intervene," I told my Keeper with a nod of my head in the direction of the two, but Naramat overrode my order with a staying action of his hand. He could look after this.

To the young whelp he asked, "Do you have a horse?"

"A fine charger, sire, with a big bold heart."

"Ride out of town now then, I pray thee, sir."

"Not until I've slayed myself a dragon."

"Ride it out of town *now* before it becomes roast meat," Naramat hissed.

"The life of a horse means little to me, sir. I can always buy another one as brave, I have no doubt. I quest for a dragon, sir. I have *come* for a dragon, sir, and shall not leave till I have slayed it."

"And shall not leave," I heard Naramat murmur, for we had all grown quiet, watching this confrontation unfold. It wasn't the first time.

"Trying to impress a young woman, are you? A test of your manhood, is it? Or are you questing for a knighthood, perhaps? So be it. You shall meet your dragon if you ride north of this tavern and take the road up the mountain. Go now, and prepare yourself!"

The whelp removed himself from our presence. Naramat rose from the table and returned his empty goblet to me. He seemed weary, done in.

"I grow tired of the jousting," was what he told me. "With luck I may come back by nightfall." With that he set off after the youth.

*

When he returned, he returned alone, and as he gave me a gold coin (the young fool's gold, I have no doubt) he said, "I don't suppose you have need of a horse by any chance? A fine charger with a bold heart, and only a slightly singed tail. It, at least, was saved."

"A horse costs money, Naramat," I said, filling his goblet for him. "And I don't travel any further than my feet will carry me anyway." I was better at being practical than accepting generous gifts; besides, he could make himself a lot of money selling a horse like that, singed tail and all.

He sat at the bar and took his time over his drink as always.

"Faith sir!" I chided when the silence between us had stretched too long, "You seem more despondent than when you left!"

"Yet I feel more light-hearted. Will you sleep with me tonight?"

I surely blushed at that. Fancy! Me! A woman who had seen more of life and its makings than many others.

"It's been a long time …" I began, looking at him as a young girl does her betrothed.

"For me also," he replied. "But we are friends, you and I; and I, at least, would love some mortal company tonight, dear lady."

"We'll see," I said, but my heart said *yes*!

As if to nudge us along, the last two customers bade me farewell and headed out into the night. But there was still work to be done …

Keeper emerged from the backroom and slanted a glance at Naramat standing next to me in the otherwise empty tavern.

"I can lock up," the big man offered. He had an alcove in the room behind the bar where he slept.

So that night I took Naramat to my bed chamber, and he laid with me till morning.

When I awoke, I was alone, though the residual warmth of his closeness was there, and my mind sang of the sweet new memories we'd made together the previous night. Exactly when he stole away from me I do not know and do not care, for I looked around my room and knew he had neither looted nor pilfered. We were friends, he and I; it might take weeks or months, but I would see him again. What happened after that remained to be seen.

And if I'd ever doubted the true nature of the man who'd bedded me so tenderly, there beside me on the pillow were a few small, delicate scales of greenish-blue colour and leathery texture.

'Everybody Wants To Be St George' was published in Dragon's Dreaming, *1985.*

Mug

Johnny Harrier fished in his jumpsuit pocket for his debit card, put it in the beverage vending machine and ordered coffee: strong, black, sweetened.

The boiling hot brew arrived in a thin plastic cup.

From previous attempts, Johnny knew better than to try to consume the liquid straight away. Instead he blew on it with all the gusto of a mini-tornado as he walked back to his seat. Reseated, he took an experimental sip and scalded his tongue yet again. Still too hot. He sat the plastic cup in the holder of the chair's armrest and sighed.

He had the bleary-eyed look of a long-distance space traveller determined to do it in comfort, if not in style, the next time he travelled.

The on-board entertainment channel was showing that infomercial about the souvenir mugs with *Andromeda Spaceways* printed on them. Sturdy things. Reliable. Not like the vending machine variety.

Johnny reached for his coffee, hoping it would be cool enough to drink by now. This time he managed to get a gulp, a much-needed hit of caffeine to his system, before the bottom of his cup began to dissolve.

In a surging mass, the contents seemed to boil and bubble in mid-air as the ship's over-zealous cleaning nanites descended like a swarm of invisible bees to stop the coffee from spilling onto the floor before it could wet or stain it.

Johnny swore quietly as the last of the cup disappeared into thin air. When he'd earlier flagged down one of the ship's crew and asked about the problem, he'd been told it was a slight technical glitch that made the nanites overanxious to clean up, and had he ever considered buying an *Andromeda Spaceways* souvenir mug? The nanites were guaranteed not to attack those.

Naturally the souvenir mugs were expensive. And if Johnny had had that sort of money to splash around, he wouldn't be travelling in steerage class—the second lowest class you could get on this ship. The lowest class was storage class. What it said was what you got: you spent your trip down in the storage hangars with the luggage and the freight. In storage, Johnny had heard, each seat came with a pair of pedals to which you were strapped and expected to use to help power the ship's engines.

Johnny Harrier sighed a low, drawn-out, moaning sigh. He wasn't conscious of doing so, but those poor souls sitting with him, trying to sleep while sitting bolt-upright in their ergonomically designed and incredibly uncomfortable seats, turned and looked at him and frowned. A few of the more outgoing ones actually hissed "Sssshhh!" at him before turning back to watch the latest informercial playing on their screens.

Holy Quasars! They were playing that *Andromeda Spaceways* mug commercial again!

Johnny wanted one of those mugs more than just about anything, except maybe to reach his destination and get off this damned uncomfortable ship. He'd give just about anything for more than just one mouthful of good, strong coffee!

He gazed longingly at the advertised mug. He hadn't allowed for such an extravagance when working out his travel budget.

Even the price of the on-board coffee was more than he'd bargained for, but some things you just couldn't travel without. If only he could have afforded to travel second class, where—according to the *ASIM* propaganda—"A selection of complimentary beverages is provided for your enjoyment".

He considered his right leg, idly wondering if *Andromeda Spaceways* dealt in used body parts. He wasn't planning on using it much for the rest of the flight; he could always hop or crawl to the food dispensers, and he could get another one grown back on later. Or maybe he could offer them a kidney as collateral? Anything so he could buy a sturdy souvenir mug and drink a full cup of coffee! His body was crying out for more caffeine!

His thoughts were disturbed by someone new and exotic entering the steerage class compartment.

She (Johnny had been fooled before, but he thought it was a 'she') wore a battered top hat, from under which metallic silver hair shot out in all directions. Reflective sunglasses (now why in blue blazes would you need those on a space ship? Johnny wondered) hid her eyes from view.

The plunging neckline of her multi-coloured dress gave a good account of one of the prettiest pairs of mammaries Johnny had ever encountered, while the broad zig-zag hem of her dress gave a good view of a pair of unfettered legs.

She caught sight of Johnny sitting in his aisle seat and strode right up to him, bold as brass. She casually lifted one of her legs, resting it on the armrest of his seat, and the hem of her dress slid obligingly up her thigh.

Johnny swallowed hard, reminded that it had been at least a month since he'd last eaten real meat.

"Hi Sugar. My name's Fleet. I was wondering if you'd care to buy a little merchandise?"

Johnny gulped. He hadn't budgeted for that either!

"I've got an authentic *Andromeda Spaceways* mug here that I'm selling really cheap."

Johnny sighed his relief while Fleet fished in a large handbag she had slung over one shoulder. The mug she produced shone enticingly in the artificial light of steerage class.

Johnny wondered if he was hallucinating due to caffeine deficiency. His prayers had been answered! Why was she holding the mug at that peculiar angle, though? Still, he could read 'Andro' on part of the mug and 'ways' embossed on the porcelain. Porcelain. Not thin, flimsy plastic. Nirvana!

"H-h-h—how much do you want for it?" Johnny panted nervously, wondering if she'd be prepared to trade in used body parts.

Fleet pulled in closer to him, like a barracuda ready to bite, and Johnny hunkered lower down in his seat for protection.

"How much have you got?" she hissed in his ear.

Johnny dived for his credit card, buried deep in his pocket, and checked the readout, quickly trying to reassess his budget.

"I can offer you 25." It was half the recommended retail price for the mug, but he hoped for the best.

"What about the rest?" Fleet asked, checking the total of credits left on the card.

"What's the point of buying a non-disintegrating mug if I then can't afford to put coffee in it?"

As Fleet seemed to ponder this, the doors to Steerage class slid open again and two burly *Andromeda Spaceways* Security guards entered.

"I'll take it!" Fleet said hurriedly as Johnny caught his first glance of the guards.

With expert fingers, Fleet pulled at a long chain around her neck. From the mysterious depths of her dress, probably in the vicinity of her navel, she produced a sales locket and inserted Johnny's debit card into its slot.

The miniaturised cash converter took a few seconds to process the transaction. All the while Fleet chanted, "Turn green, turn green, turn green!" A green light blinked on the converter indicating Johnny's money was now credited to her account. Throwing Johnny's card and his mug into his lap, Fleet said, "Bye!" before taking off towards the back of the compartment.

Funny how legs with that much meat on them could move so fast, Johnny reflected.

His normal razor-sharp reactions somewhat delayed by recent lack of caffeine and sleep, Johnny Harrier fingered his non-disintegrating mug as if it were the Holy Grail. Squinting, he read each letter of the logo. *ANDROGYNOUS SPICEWAYS.* Something wasn't quite right there, but he was yet to fathom what it was.

While he puzzled over the mug, the long arm of the law, or in this case the fat hand of an *Andromeda Spaceways* Security guard descended upon him.

Johnny stared bleary eyed into a chest far more formidable than his own, where the letters 'A.S.S.' assaulted his eyes in day-glow letters. Johnny felt he was about to become part of a bar brawl, and the last time that happened was the last time he'd eaten meat.

"Excuse me, sir," drawled the bulky security guard. "But you seem to be in possession of illegal contraband."

Johnny frowned, then realised the guard was referring to the mug.

"If you wouldn't mind getting out of your seat nice and slow like so that we aren't forced to do something we really don't want to."

They didn't look like they didn't want to. They looked like they wanted to very much. With spikes.

Fluidly and majestically, Johnny Harrier unfolded himself from his seat—then beat the hell out of there, glad that he'd decided not to trade his right leg after all.

He hared off after the shyster saleswoman, determined to give her a piece of his mind.

The two security guards followed hot on his heels once they'd finally realised what was going on. Fortunately for Johnny, they were rarely employed for their lightning speed, either physical or mental.

Funny how adrenalin can make you feel more alive than caffeine, Johnny thought as he bounded away, leaving the guards a good distance behind him. His athletic prowess brought scattered applause from around steerage class—anything that broke the monotony of a long-distance flight had to be a good thing.

Johnny was surprised when he emerged from Steerage class onto a rickety catwalk stretched across a dark void that seemed to drop away forever.

Swift, but not stupid, Fleet had slowed down to carefully navigate the catwalk. Johnny soon caught up with her.

"Where did all this extra space come from?" Johnny wondered, one hand gripping the handrail as he looked all around him.

"Matt paintings. Trust me, I'm an artist." Johnny noticed that Fleet was also holding the handrail, not quite hard enough to leave her fingerprints embedded in the metal, but close. She was panting for breath too.

"What's wrong with you?" Johnny asked.

"I said my name was Fleet, not Fit," she replied.

"Where are we?"

"Storage class," Fleet puffed.

Hoping to catch a glimpse of those poor souls travelling in Storage class, Johnny leaned out over the handrail as far as he dared and looked down. He thought he heard moaning, a whip cracking and the sound of a multitude of pedals from the darkness far below.

"Stop right there!" an A.S.S. guard shouted.

Johnny jerked back sharply at the sound of the guard's voice and his *Androgynous Spiceways* mug slipped out of his jumpsuit pocket. As if in slow motion it spun base over apex, his fingers fumbling to grasp it securely once more.

Fleet's hand also launched itself to grab the mug, and their hands met, cradling the mug safely between them. Though she was still wearing reflective sunglasses, Johnny got the impression that she was staring deeply into his eyes. It unnerved him.

"Phew, that was close!" Johnny breathed.

"You're under arrest!" the second guard called.

In a muted voice, out of the corner of his mouth, Johnny asked Fleet, "What do we do?"

"Let them capture us," Fleet replied, already holding her hands up.

"What?" Johnny was incredulous. "Then why did you run away in the first place?"

"Company."

"Company?"

"Trust me."

If there was one thing Johnny Harrier had learned in his adventures through time and space, it was not to trust anyone who said, "Trust me," but he didn't seem to have a choice.

"We're taking you to the brig!"

They were led back through Storage Class, Steerage Class, Economy and Second Class. Johnny's eyes bulged wider as he took in all the luxurious appointments and fittings, getting better and better in each consecutive class. In second class they actually had inviting, comfortable seats! They called to him, trying to entice him to sit on them as he passed. And a complimentary beverage counter (they said they liked his brown eyes!), offering as much tea, coffee of a variety of other refreshments, all served in practical ceramic cups with the correct *Andromeda Spacceways* logo embossed upon them that you didn't even have to pay for!

Finally they were being hauled into First Class.

"What's this?" Johnny asked, hesitating on the threshold of a spacious and luxurious First Class cabin, the kind you only saw in the *Andromeda Spaceways* infomercials.

"None of the *Andromeda Spaceways* ships have brigs," Fleet explained to Johnny in a low voice. "But they do all have First Class cabins, which are rarely booked on account of them being so unaffordable, so one doubles as the other."

The guards shoved them into the cabin and locked the door behind them.

Johnny thought if this was prison then it wasn't so bad, but then he saw Fleet sprawled on the one and only bed in the cabin and had second thoughts. The silver haired temptress patted the mattress invitingly. Johnny got the impression that she also winked at him from behind her sunglasses. He got very worried. The only thing he fancied doing on the bed right now involved sleeping, and he suspected having him snoring blissfully in her ear was not what Fleet had in mind.

"Some pieces of trivia are worth knowing," she informed him.

Intent on keeping as much distance between Fleet and himself as he could for the moment, Johnny explored the rest of his luxurious confines. There was a fully stocked minibar and a spacious ensuite bathroom. Tastefully appointed gold-plated fixtures gleamed at him. Complimentary toiletries, including those nifty little plastic shower caps, were artfully arranged above a marble sink. There was a choice of sonic or water shower, and a round hot tub dominated the room. Bliss! Now this really was travelling, Johnny thought.

"Do they supply coffee?" Johnny asked hopefully from the middle of the luxurious bathroom.

In reply, Fleet opened a bedside wood-grain cabinet. Filterbags and pods of coffee beckoned to Johnny to come sample. The faint aromas of coffee beans roasted on exotic planets all over the galaxy insinuated themselves in his sinuses and he started to drool all over again.

In a state of rapture, Johnny took a careless step forward, slipped on a build-up of soap scum the on-board nanites had pointedly left there in protest of them not receiving higher wages, and fell heavily on his rear end.

The Androgynous Spiceways mug leaped from his jumpsuit pocket like a dolphin released from captivity. It rose in a high, wide arc before plummeting onto the tiled floor where it shattered into a dozen pieces.

Johnny stared at the shards of mug in stunned disbelief, then he looked hopefully to Fleet for solace, or at least a replacement.

She shrugged and smiled. "Sorry, that was the last one."

"But the coffee-making supplies ... surely?"

Fleet checked the wood grain cabinet again. "There's plenty of those flimsy plastic cups; you know, the ones the nanites consume before you've had a chance to finish your drink?"

The First Class hallways on the *Andromeda Spaceways* ship echoed the deep-seated but eerie cry as Johnny Harrier howled.

'Mug' was first published in issue 2 of Andromeda Spaceways Inflight Magazine, *August 2002. Editor: Robbie Matthews.*

I was pleased to be a founding member of the Andromeda Spaceways *publishing co-operative. One of our original aims was to publish stories from the lighter side of the spec-fic spectrum. Submissions were read 'blind'—no details of who the author was, so the story was gauged on its merits alone.* ASIM *also had a rotating editorship, each co-op member taking a turn at editing an issue, which I believe allowed for a wider spectrum of stories to be selected, as every editor had varying tastes.* ASIM *reminded me of my passion for editing, and gave me the experience and confidence to get training as a professional editor. I stuck with* Andromeda Spaceways *for 13 years. The early years in particular were fun-filled. The original co-op, and the many who joined and left after, made a wonderfully diversified, talented group. As their token hobby ceramicist, I produced a limited edition of* Andromeda Spaceways *mugs to raise money for the co-op, and had a great time spoofing myself in this story. Though all of the original members have left now, the magazine continues to be published by a younger, fresher team. Long may she sail!*

Divorce

Dear Maurice,

I'm leaving you.

I think I was a good and dutiful wife to you during the years we were married. I took you for richer or poorer. I've loved you in sickness and in health, I have done almost all I can do to satisfy you, though I admit that in return you've been an almost flawless husband.

You aren't messy. You don't leave your clothes draped on the floor. You don't get drunk and come home late, though if you did I'd make good use of that marble rolling pin your mother gave me as a wedding present! To the best of my knowledge you've been faithful to me. You don't snore. You don't smoke. You've cooked just as many meals for me as I have for you. You're a good lover ... you're a very good lover. You're kind and considerate. You never forget my birthday, or our anniversary, and you surprise me with flowers and chocolates at least four times a year whether I deserve them or not.

In short, my dearest Maurice, you are the sweetest, most considerate man I have ever met or could ever hope to meet. I love you just as much as I did on our wedding day, if not more so.

But I'm filing for a divorce.

The one problem affecting the stability of our relationship started off as a small one, Maurice dear, but oh how it's grown!

You wanted a pet, you said, all of 18 months ago. Not a cat, or a dog, a budgie or a goldfish, or something considered 'normal', mind! Not an okapi, or an elephant, tiger, polar bear or beaver. Or something else exotic. Not a dodo, a mermaid, a satyr or a unicorn, or something as gently eccentric.

No! You had to be the first (and the only one for obvious reasons) on the block to have a pet dragon.

Yes, I admit it was sort of cute when it first came out of its shell, if something taller at birth than a great dane, and twice as heavy, can be considered cute. And yes, Maurice, I agree that it didn't give us much bother at first. For the first two minutes of its life at least, it was helpless and harmless. But oh, for the rest of it!

If you really want to know, no I wasn't terribly impressed with its endearing gurglings on bath days. Remember how it thought our gold-plated gargoyle taps were its own personal rubber ducks?

You started bathing it in the pool after that. Remember how I'd longed to own a house with a pool, Maurice? Remember how I use to go swimming every morning winter or summer to keep my body trim, taut and terrific—just the way you liked it, Maurice? Remember how you laughed off my complaints about the pool water acquiring a fishy odour after it became your dragon's bathtub? Or the purple spots I broke out in when I dared to swim in that tainted water?

Don't you recall the fun we had when your dragon caught a cold? The local fire-brigade was on stand-by for weeks! And they had to rush around and put the fire out every time your dragon sneezed. We're still paying off the cost of fire-proofing the neighbours' homes, not to mention ours.

Then there's the basic problem of feeding the thing. Do you know just how much of our combined salary is taken up just to keep that pet of yours fed each week?

I haven't bought myself a new dress since that thing got here, what with food bills, repair bills, and trying to put off law suits from people who have encountered your pet dragon.

No, Maurice, they aren't 'just jealous' dear! I somehow doubt that it's only because they want one as a pet too.

Yes, I know he's affectionate. I still have the bruises from the last 'hug' he gave me and the stitches from his last 'playful swipe' aren't due to come out until next Thursday.

And in case it's slipped your mind, poor old Mrs Vanderhurst had a stroke when your dragon 'smiled' at her. She's still in rehabilitation, but at least her ability to talk has come back, even if the only thing she has managed to mutter so far is, "All those TEETH. All those TEETH," over and over again; but the nurses say she's making progress.

Before I forget, there was someone here today from the cattle yards. It seems that when your dragon last slipped his leash he flew over there for a quick snack. You owe them two bullocks.

Oh, and the air traffic authorities phoned up today as well. Yes, while off on one of his little jaunts, your dragon decided to play 'tag' with a couple of jets.

Well, don't look at me. I was the one who told you to get his wings clipped, but would you listen? No! You said a dragon wasn't a dragon if he couldn't fly.

There's just one other thing, Maurice: your dragon seems to have developed a case of diarrhoea. He's been off colour most of the day, just resting in his roost. Do you remember when his roost used to be our roof?

I suggest you clear up after him—after all he is *your* pet. Better do it before the roof caves in from an excess of dragon 'doo-doo'.

God only knows what you're going to do to clear the smell! I've only survived so far by using a gas mask. It's guaranteed against mustard gas, nerve gas and tear gas, but it doesn't quite keep the full effects of dragon gas at bay!

The neighbours will no doubt complain, and you can expect to hear from the state pollution authorities. If they mention a low lying cloud of smog blanketing the city on the weather report tonight, you-know-who is to blame.

For peace of mind, I've taken the phone off the hook and not answered the door. He's your dragon, you handle the problem for once.

As for me, well, Maurice darling, I'll be seeing you in court. I want half the furniture and half the photos, but under no circumstances do I want custody of *your* dragon!

Your dinner is in the oven.

Love,
Alice.

'Divorce' was published in Andromeda Spaceways Inflight Magazine *Issue 4, 2002. Editor: Tehani Croft.*

White

They'd dressed her up as an angel for the midnight pageant that Christmas. The deep red of her angel dress only served to highlight her pale skin and her fair hair that sat softly around her face like a halo of spun gold.

Cathy had tried to be an especially good girl all year, and her one Christmas wish, shared with so many children around the world, was to be allowed to feel the sunlight on her face and not be mauled by its damaging rays.

How often had Mr Wong told her? Everywhere now, but especially here in Australia, the sun was like a tiger: so graceful in its movements and so beautiful to look at from a safe distance, but it was deadly. And if you were exposed to its full strength, it could kill you in just a few minutes. Like the tiger, the sun was waiting to gobble you up.

Mr Wong kept a tiger in his expansive subterranean compound. Cathy was allowed to visit the tiger whenever she wanted, just so long as she kept to the viewing areas and out of its domain. It was a black and white striped tiger, more rare than its black and gold striped cousins. Not a true albino, Mr Wong had explained to her; a genetic flaw gave these tigers their unusual pelts and beautiful blue eyes. It wasn't known if there were any of these tigers still living in the wild. If the poachers hadn't already wiped them out, possibly the sun had taken its toll, as it had for people and animals all around the world.

Those who could afford it, like Mr Wong, had vowed to protect samples of as many species as they could in the hope of one day being able to breed up stock and return them to the wild. Modern day Noahs, their arks were carved in subterranean compounds protected by wide sails of shade cloth, rather than wood to float on the flood tides.

The tiger's domain was heavily shaded by trees that in turn were protected by a tinted PVC dome that screened out most of the harmful UV rays.

Mr Wong kept other animals too for his enjoyment. In a massive aviary complex he kept and bred white doves of peace, sulphur crested cockatoos, storks, ducks and even Northern Hemisphere white swans (their native counterparts, the black swans, didn't appeal to him.). A few white cattle, sheep and rare albino wallabies were presided over by a white Andalusian stallion that had a noble but gentle disposition.

Cathy had been taught to ride on the stallion's wide back. Supervised, of course, in a round ring with thick white walls.

What a spectacle they made as they went around and around the ring, Cathy's hair almost the same colour as the horse's, streaming behind her as the horse's mane and tail flew out behind it, white on white on white as the walls of the ring became a white blur. Cathy used to think that if it wasn't for the colour of her clothes and the horse's gear, and the lunge rope, no one would see them except as a white smudge against a white wall.

The horse's name was Cascade because its mane and tail reminded Mr Wong of falling water.

Cathy had been with Mr Wong and his family since she was three years old. She only had vague memories of what life with her parents had been like despite them sending her recordings and presents every Christmas and for her birthday. She vaguely knew that Mr Wong had promised her parents that he'd give her the best schooling, the best lifestyle and the best protection from the sun that money could buy, when he took her in to his own family.

His charming wife, Mama Wong (Cathy could never bring herself to call her just "Mum" or "Mother") was kind and gentle, and his two daughters—Ming Ming and May Lee—treated Cathy like their little sister. They were fun-loving girls, full of laughter. Grandma Tse, Mrs Wong's mother, also lived with them.

With the staff members who shared the compound—Jimmy, Laura and Mrs Entwhistle, the cook—Cathy had all the family she would ever need.

Life was wonderful under the care of her wealthy benefactor, far better than it would have been if she had to live outside where the sun, like a tiger, would have gobbled her up in no time because of her fair complexion.

Mr Wong had explained it all to her in great detail, and his daughters kept reinforcing the unwritten law. The sun was a dangerous hunter, and you never, never ventured into its domain.

Sometimes Mr Wong would disregard his own rules. Cathy would see him out walking in the dusty paddocks that surrounded their compound, bathed in the hazy gold and orange hues of sunrise or sunset. But he was older, he explained. His skin had been conditioned to the harsh environment.

Grandma Tse had stubbornly lived in her high-rise seaside apartment in Surfers Paradise until the rising sea had ripped away her beloved beach front and she'd had to move inland. She was old enough to remember and love a gentler sunshine. She came from a time when people worked and played in the daylight and let it be their friend. That was many years ago before everyone knew better.

Despite taking all the precautions, like wearing hats, sunscreens and long-sleeved garments, as well as staying out of the sun during the hottest part of the day, skin cancers—like vindictive flowers—bloomed on her face as if she were a garden bed. Frequently they had to be picked out. Her body was lined with scars from past harvests and skin grafts.

"You don't want to be like me, do you?" she'd warn the girls seriously.

And they'd shake their heads earnestly, knowing how lucky they were to be protected from the sun.

But then they'd ask her for stories of what it was like living in reverse to the way they lived. What was it like waking at dawn instead of dusk, living in sunlight instead of living by the softer, safer moonlight and starshine? The world Grandma Tse had grown up in seemed alien and endlessly fascinating to the girls.

Cathy watched through the thick treated glass of her bedroom window as Mr Wong walked among the few tortured eucalyptus trees that grew in an expansive paddock outside her room. The hum of the air conditioners whirred in the background like a mechanical swarm of flies. She'd been awake since mid-afternoon, restless and full of anticipation, the way she'd been on Christmas Eve a week ago.

Now as she watched Mr Wong gently bathed in the departing rays of the sun, she remembered what it had been that had tugged at her spirit. This was the last day of the year, New Year's Eve.

For all her life she had heard about the promise that had been made by the governments of the world some fifty years earlier. If the people of the world agreed to trade night for day, they would save themselves from the threat of dying early deaths from skin cancer, and the other cancers and sicknesses that had arisen from the destruction of the ozone layer . By that stage even those living in temperate climates were not immune. So the world had traded sunlight for moonlight, those that could afford it swapping skyscrapers for the safety of subterranean buildings, or cave systems. All the rest making do with what shelter they could find.

And those with fair-haired, beautiful children like Cathy, who weren't able to bring them up sheltered away from the harsh sun, tried to find sponsors who could give their children safety that the parents could not.

Now, hopefully, fifty years after the world had finally agreed (out of desperation more than common sense) to do away with the pollution and the propellants, the atmosphere might have recovered enough to allow people to safely have more exposure to daylight.

All Cathy longed for was to go to the beach and play in the sand, and see the clouds so white and fluffy in daylight, not filtered by reinforced screens.

On hot, sticky summer nights they'd all packed into the family car and driven down to the beach, a mere thirty-minute drive away from Mr Wong's compound. But even with the bright overhead lights illuminating the beach and the breakers, you could never see what might be swimming in the water with you. While the automatic buoys could sound shark alarms, there were still bluebottles, stingers and jellyfish to worry about. Everything that brushed against you in the water was a potential threat, even though it was usually only seaweed or plastic.

Grandma Tse would wear her bright swimming costume, but she would rarely venture into the water any deeper than her knees. She was always too worried about what might be lurking deeper. She always said that it had been so much nicer to be at the beach during daylight hours when you could see into the water.

When the curfew was lifted, the family told Cathy, when it was safe to spend more time out in the daylight again, they would come to the beach then, and Cathy could see for herself how pretty the clouds and waves looked in daylight. But she would still have to be very, very careful to wear sunscreen, hat and clothing to protect her faint skin, and to only stay in the sun for a little while lest it try to gobble her up like a tiger.

Cathy didn't care. She'd wear a hat and sunscreen and anything else, just so long as she could feel the sunshine on her face, see the ocean as blue instead of grey and black, and see the fluffy clouds not tainted by night or tinted windows.

The announcement would be made at midnight, she'd been told. After that the New Year's celebrations would really begin. The family had planned a picnic feast at dawn to finally be able to greet the sun unshielded. It was going to be even better than Christmas!

As darkness crept across the land, Cathy watched through one of the tinted windows as Mr Wong turned the Andalusian stallion and the albino wallabies out to graze in a paddock. What little grass was growing there was tough and shrivelled, determined to grow despite exposure to a belligerent sun. The animals picked, not that any of them had need for food. Mr Wong spent a small fortune on his menagerie, buying the best hay, chaff, grains and seeds cultivated under protective domes. The only foodstuffs that grew well unprotected were those kept mostly in shade at the bottom of steep-sided valleys.

The moon, nearly full on this new year, rose and shed its gentle light across the landscape. In the paddock, the horse glowed incandescently where the moonbeams caressed its hide.

Maybe tomorrow, Cathy thought. Maybe tomorrow I'll ride you to the beach and we'll splash in the white waves under the white clouds. She imagined the sight they'd make, the stallion's long mane and tail flowing, her fair hair streaming behind her as they galloped along the sand, splashed through the white foaming breakers. She'd been inspired to do this by a film clip she'd seen taken in the time before, when it was still safe to be out in daylight, and she'd been desperate to live the scene ever since.

With darkness safely upon the land, family and friends began arriving in their electric cars, keen to be together to celebrate the expected news. Cathy hoped they'd let her stay up until dawn once the all-clear was announced, so she could stand with the rest of them, out in the open and greet the new sun.

As midnight got closer, the raucous party became quieter and people gathered around the television sets. The traditional midnight display of fireworks was broadcast to celebrate the arrival of the New Year and everyone drank champagne. Then the Prime Minister's image appeared on their screens. Australia would be among the first to hear the global announcement. Voices dropped to whispers, then conversations fell away all together.

The Prime Minister spoke at length about how the problems of ozone depletion had led to everyone in the world drastically altering how they lived their lives fifty years ago. Cathy squirmed impatiently in her seat. She didn't understand a lot of the big words, she was just waiting to hear that her Christmas wish had been granted and that they could all go down to the beach during daylight. She was aware that as the woman on the big screen spoke the mood of those around her in the room was becoming more sombre.

"And so it is with deep regret that I must inform you that despite our concerted efforts, we have not been able to revive the ozone layer. For our own protection, therefore, it has been decided that we as a nation and as a planet, will have to continue with our current arrangements for at least another fifty years ..."

There might have been more, but the disappointed noises from those at the party drowned them out. People started consoling each other, airing their own opinions. While she mightn't have understood every word the Prime Minister had said, Cathy got the general meaning from the reactions of those around her. There would be no dawn picnic to greet the sun. And she'd have to wait forever for the next chance to enjoy daylight without hiding behind a thick, domed shield. Cathy started to cry.

Grandma Tse hurried to pat the child's hand to comfort her while Mr Wong, Mama Wong, Ming Ming and May Lee all grouped around their little angel and tried to soothe her. She could tell by their troubled eyes and heavy hearts that she was not the only one to be disappointed.

In the cool pre-dawn hours they put her to bed in the hope that sleep would ease the anguish of the night for Cathy.

But she stayed wide awake to watch another daring dawn invade the darkened sky. Cathy was angry at being deprived of this daylight, when everyone had told her that it would happen; today she was determined to live her dream.

Quietly she made her way out to the stallion's stable. She shushed his whickered welcome and pulled his head low to fit his bridle. By standing on the tack box, she was able to put the saddle on his back. He'd been taught to stand passively while all this occurred.

Using all her strength, Cathy tightened the saddle's girth strap and stood on the tack box again to climb into the saddle.

With a clatter of hooves they were through the open stable door, up the ramp and out into the paddock and the birth of a new day, a day that Cathy was determined to have. She would not be denied the surf in sunlight any longer.

The stallion's contained strength rippled underneath Cathy as she rode the horse out into the raw light. For a while she was cautious, making Cascade walk when she knew he wanted to run. He snorted in the sweet warm air. Where she could, Cathy kept the horse protected by what sparse shade the surrounding withered, twisted trees offered, but nothing dangerous was happening. The sun did not pounce on them like a tiger.

Unable to turn to sleep to quash his disappointment, Mr Wong rose from his bed where he'd rested fully clothed, and went wandering in his compound. He wanted to look in on the pale little girl he cared for like a daughter. Last night's announcement had troubled her greatly. She didn't expect adults to go back on their word.

Surprised to find her bed was empty, he began to search the rest of his compound, hoping to find her and to explain to her why things were the way they were.

When Mr Wong found the stallion gone, his bridle and saddle also missing, he feared the worst and raised the household. If they were quick they could find Cathy and bring her home before she was harmed.

At first Cathy giggled as the sun tickled her. She urged the stallion to a stylish trot, then a rocking canter as she drank in the scenery around her. Dry and brittle in the summer heat, the landscape seemed more intense than it ever was by nightlight.

Grandma Tse had been right, the colours *were* brighter in daylight!

And the sky was so *big* and *blue*! You never got the proper colour looking at the sky through tinted windows and screens.

The light breeze that had kept her cool dropped away and the sun's tickling rays became sharp needle-pricks of heat.

Cascade had started to sweat from running, but now Cathy felt sweat trickle down her brow, her back, and through her jeans too.

She reined the horse to a halt and glanced back behind her towards Mr Wong's compound. The sensible thing would be to return to the safety she had always known there. Mr Wong was a gentle man who would forgive her impetuousness.

She looked forward. To see the ocean by daylight! That had been her only Christmas wish. The governments should have kept their promises.

Cascade marked time, impatient to get going one way or the other. He had plenty of energy left. Maybe if they galloped all the way they'd make it to the sea?

With a nudge of her heels in his ribs, the stallion was in flight. The scenery hurtled past them, but Cathy kept her eyes straight ahead, looking for a sign of the sea.

The sun kept climbing towards its zenith, like a tiger prowling through its terrain.

It all depended on them conducting their search *thoroughly*, Mr Wong told his people. They had two cars they could use. The compound's roustabout offered maximum protection from the sun for at least one hour, while the saloon that he used for business trips and family outings would offer full protection for maybe half an hour longer.

"Cathy said she was looking forward to going to the beach in daylight." Ming Ming supplied a possible clue as to where they might find the little girl.

"Poor child, poor child, poor child," Grandma Tse muttered over and over again as she wrung her hands, her eyes wide with worry and staring at nothing while she imagined the child's fate.

Mr Wong had diplomatically suggested she stay at home in case Cathy returned. Grandma Tse's old, scarred skin was more susceptible to sunlight after all her years of exposure, and he sought to protect her.

Split into two groups, they set out in the two cars to find Cathy.

It had been a little over an hour since Cathy's adventure had begun to turn against her. All around them the horizon was obscured by a shimmering heat haze. Cascade's pace had slowed to a reluctant walk. The heat blazed down from the sun and reflected up from the hard, parched ground. It felt like being in a furnace.

Cathy's skin was red and sore, and already blistering in parts. Her clothes offered little protection, she could feel her skin burning despite their cover. Her head was swimming and she felt sick.

It was futile. There was no sign of the ocean ahead. She thought if only she could bathe in its bright blue waves she might be spared.

Water. All she wanted was water, but she hadn't thought to bring anything to drink.

Surrendering to defeat, she urged the horse to some scraggly trees that at least offered a little shade. There she slid from the saddle and pressed her back against a tree trunk. Even the bark was hot, and what shade was on offer was only slightly cooler than being in the sun. She looped the stallion's reins around her wrist for fear that he would wander off. But he wasn't going anywhere. His head hung low as he panted in heat distress. He moved his weight from one leg to another as if the ground burnt his hooves.

"Don't die," Cathy whimpered to him as she patted his long face. "Please Cascade, don't die."

Then, panting and dehydrated, she slipped into black oblivion.

Cathy's small body was a mass of ugly red blisters when they found her. She remembered being wrapped in cool, wet sheets, but not much more.

She teetered between life and death for weeks, crying out through the painful but necessary treatment. The drugs they gave her helped erase the memory of the pain, but not the pain itself. She never forgot the Andalusian stallion though.

When she finally found the courage to ask what had happened to Cascade, Grandma Tse tried to explain it to her gently. The horse could not fit into the car. And they'd been so anxious to get Cathy to safety, it would not have been able to keep up with the speeding car no matter how fast it ran. They'd had to leave it out all day to try and fend for itself the best way it could. When Mr Wong had gone back out to retrieve the horse that evening it was too late. The sun, like a tiger, had gobbled it up.

Mr Wong was heartbroken, though he did his best to hide it. The horse had meant a lot to him. He'd been counting on the stallion to help re-establish a breeding empire when—if—the curfew was ever lifted and the world returned to normal. Too late now, too late. Even if the horse had not been sacrificed to the sun, Mr Wong knew Cascade wouldn't have lived another fifty years. Maybe there could have been a breeding program, he was in contact with a couple of people who owned mares. They'd been in discussions when they thought the curfew might be lifted. But now, when the earth had not healed, discussion had dried up.

Cathy had been mauled by the sun. Some of her beautiful fair hair had been burnt away, some had fallen out through stress. The doctors assured her it would grow back in time, but the angel's halo had been singed. Her skin was patches of red upon red upon red, except for the patches of skin that were white. She would never again have skin of translucent beauty, never again have a 'peaches and cream' complexion.

Each year of her life would be marked by trips to skin specialists who were already warning her that skin cancers would be inevitable, probably for the rest of her life.

So, like Grandma Tse, her skin would come to resemble a quilt made up of patches of skin grafts and scars.

Cathy lost her innocence that day. Their Christmas angel had fallen and become mortal. She would never long to be in the sun again, would never see the beach by daylight, no matter if she lived to see the curfew lifted.

Sometimes she would sit and gaze for hours at the thick white walls of the compound's riding ring where she'd been taught to ride, and she'd remember a girl and a horse blending white against white against white, until they were barely indistinguishable from those incandescent walls.

We seem to have averted the post-apocalyptic world caused by the degradation of the ozone layer that I imagined more than 20 years ago. I'm glad I got this one wrong.

I Saw A Man Upon The Stair

I saw a man upon a stair, a homeless man. Or did he call the street his home? Or the stair where he tended to camp? He seemed so organised. His life contained in a cart, off which hung a lot of canvas bags. And when I dwelled on it, I recalled I'd seen him on this patch over a number of years. I was seeing him more frequently these days because my new job was in his neighbourhood.

People like me—with roofs over our heads—tend to make the assumption that people like him—the Man Upon The Stair—make the choice to live the way they do, to be suburban Bedouin.

As winter settled in, I used to wonder more about him. Where did he go to get out of the rain? How did he keep himself warm of a night? I'd noticed a camp bed set up on the topmost step, but was that enough? The wind can whistle cold around the city canyons. Did he push his cart to a hostel on nights like that? Did the Lifeline van hunt him down like a dog-collector pursuing a stray dog to offer him hot soup and conversation?

I'd noticed people talking to him from time to time as I'd hurried past, keen to catch my bus, and I'd thought to myself, "Oh, he must be alright. He has people watching out for him."

We made eye contact from time to time, acknowledged each other's alien existence.

I'd even fantasize about befriending him eventually, but I come from an abusive past, and you've got to be so careful these days.

You don't know when you're likely to be abused or attacked, even by homeless men in the streets. And poverty is a contagious disease. I didn't want to catch it.

I saw a man upon a stair, and when I looked he was not there. Followed the sunshine north, I surmised to entertain myself as I hurried by his empty haunt. But a week or two later he was back. I was glad to see him set up camp on the stairs again. Somehow it made something right in the world.

I saw a man upon a stair, and when I looked he was not there. Well, his cart and canvas bags were gone, and the camp bed, and the plastic ponchos that he used as shelter from the rain. But in their place was a large framed photo of him, taken, I suspect, many years ago. Bunches of flowers adorned his stairs, and written respectfully in chalk were the words, "Rest In Peace, Matt."

I saw a man upon a stair, and when I looked he was not there, but clearly he had friends who cared about him. Did he think he died alone? I never got to know him, but I grieve his passing.

Published in issue 415 of The Big Issue, *September 2012.*

Earth Girls Aren't Easy

It was the Friday night of the big convention. An ice-breaking party. I was there on my own, trying not to be a wallflower, but failing miserably.

He stood in front of me and smiled. He was gorgeous. After stilted, polite conversation I said, "Look, I'm no-one special."

"But I am," he replied smoothly. "I'm from another planet."

Taking the convention theme too far? I wondered.

"So how did you get—"

"Interstellar cruiser. Parked on the roof of this very hotel."

"Bullsh—"

"Wanna go for a ride?"

If I hadn't had that third vodka and orange I might have said "No", but I was curious so I shrugged.

He took my hand and led me from the room.

His hand was up my skirt, his tongue down my throat the minute we were out on the roof-top garden. My head was clearing in the fresh air, but not fast enough. I extricated myself.

"Your spaceship?" I challenged.

"Right over there." He pressed a button on his keyring. Nothingness dissolved. A shuttle, the size of a bus, appeared before my eyes.

If I hadn't had that third vodka …

"Come on, let's go!"

"I'll be sick! All those Gs, then no gravity!"

"Old technology. Don't sweat it."

He had my hand again. The offer was too good to refuse.

The roof of the hotel drifted away from us. The city became a starscape below, the stars a cityscape above.

Going from sub-light to FTL was an experience. But when his hands came off the controls they were all over me.

"Now cut that out!" I warned, not that I could get out and walk home.

As if on command, the engines stopped whirring faintly in the background. He tried to restart them but couldn't. He tried again and I panicked.

"Where are we?"

"Four light years from Earth."

"Shit! I'm expected back at work on Tuesday! Do something." He leered.

"Do something else! Phone for road-service!"

"You know, for an Earthgirl, you make good sense."

I glared at him while he made the call.

He went for a grope. I discovered his genitals were roughly located where you'd find them on a human male, and kicking him there had the same result.

It got quiet after that. Except for his sobbing.

A repair ship arrived out of the inky blackness. It locked on to ours. The pilot came across. He looked like Harpo Marx.

After flicking a few switches, unscrewing a junction point and looking in (just to make it look like he was doing something, I suspect) he pronounced, "The ship's in a bad state. More repairs here than I can handle."

"I'll never get back to Earth!" I wailed.

"I can give you a lift."

"Be seeing you," I told my pilot and followed Harpo back through the airlock.

"You're leaving him stranded here?"

"There'll be a full repair unit with him fairly soon. He'll be fine. Earth, you said?"

"If you'd be so kind. Well, that's a few good hours wasted. I bet the party's over by now."

"My ship's got time-travel capabilities, does that help you?"

My eyebrows rose. I contemplated delight.

"Could you take me back to early Friday evening? But take your time; I'd like to get to know you better."

It was the Friday night of the big convention, an icebreaking party. Smiling confidently, I walked in on the arm of an alien who looked like Harpo Marx.

Published in Antipodean SF *issue 10 (1998). Editor: Ion Newcombe.*

Vale Douglas Adams

"Bad news" was the subject header on the email I received. The body of the email only contained a link to a BBC website, no comment, no explanation. I thought it might have something to do with *Doctor Who*; or maybe the latest effort to relaunch *Blake's 7* had failed. Instead I was confronted with the news that Douglas Adams had died.

A wormhole opened up in the space-time continuum, and I was hurtled back to the heady days of the 1980s and my first encounter with *The Hitchhikers Guide to the Galaxy*.

I discovered *Hitchhikers* as a radio play on what was then Sydney ABC middle-of-the-road radio station 2BL (now ABC 702). After it aired there, the radio play was broadcast on the hip and groovy 2JJ, meant for younger listeners of the ABC.

A science fiction comedy, a humorous science fiction work—I didn't care. It combined two of my greatest loves and I was in seventh heaven.

As enjoyable as the radio series was, it was only when someone loaned me a copy of the novelisation of the radio series that *The Guide* kicked in for me.

"I remember this!" I exclaimed, and set about not so much reading the book as devouring it.

I have, both before and after this experience, read books that I have liked enough to urge friends to read, even loaning them my copy of a book so that they might do so. But *Hitchhikers* was something different. It was like finding yourself on an alien planet, and making everyone you come into contact with learn to speak from your native dictionary. Or alternatively, it was like going around sticking a Babel fish into the ear of everyone you came across, so that they could speak the same language you did.

With the passion of a religious zealot, I thrust my copy of *The Guide* into the hands of family and friends, with orders to read, and read fast—as there were others queued up behind them to take their place.

It was a joy to discover I wasn't alone. All around the world, young people were tuning into *The Guide*. Fan clubs were soon being formed to honour the book and Douglas Adams. The British club, *ZZ9 Plural Z Alpha* was among the first, if not the first fan club to spring up. It is still thriving today, and has a global membership some 20 years after its inception.

Australia can boast at least three *Guide*-inspired fan clubs, all originating in Victoria. While ADASA (Arthur Dent Appreciation Society of Australia) and CHAS (Cosmic Hitchers Association) had affiliations with university and college campuses, the Hitchers Club of Australia, founded by the late Ian Gunn, recruited members from a wider pool. The heydays for *Hitchhikers* fandom in Australia stretched from the mid-1980s until the early 1990s.

The La Boit theatre company in Brisbane was one of a few theatre companies outside Great Britain to take on the challenge of producing *The Guide* on stage. Danny Murphy adapted the *Hitchhikers* script for the local production and the season ran for a month at the end of 1984. By then *The Hitchhikers Guide to the Galaxy* had seen life as a radio play, LP vinyl records (originally funded by Douglas Adams when the BBC saw no reason to produce them) novelisation (translated into many languages including German, Japanese, Swedish and Braille), theatre productions and a television series.

While the long-talked about *Hitchhikers* movie never saw the light of day and probably never will*, the material was certainly accessible. Later the series would be released as audio-novels, a computer game, graphic novel and trading cards.

Adams was sent on whirlwind world tours to promote *The Guide* and subsequent books, through numerous television and radio appearances as well as book signings.

As his popularity grew, he became a sought-after speaker at literary lunches and dinners. Watching and listening to Adams speak at one of these events, you might have got the distinct impression that he was as much a frustrated actor as he was a famous writer.

Adams was generous with his fans—up to a point. He would make an effort to reply to fanmail, often providing a newsletter of latest developments desktop published on one of his Apple Macs. In more recent years, he was accessible by emails via The Global Village. But while often invited to attend science fiction conventions, he would usually cordially accept the invitation, only to decline politely later.

Having written that the answer to the meaning of *Life, the Universe and Everything* was '42', he watched in bemusement as the 'cult of 42' took on a life of its own. People came up with theories and hypotheses regarding the relevance of the number, and one enterprising postgraduate student actually managed to pen a thesis on the importance of the number in various cultures.

For a time, Douglas Adams went into denial about being a science fiction writer, declaring that the *Hitchhikers* series of books (possibly the only trilogy in five parts) wasn't science fiction at all. This caused a few raised eyebrows from anyone familiar with the genre. If it *wasn't* science fiction, it was a damn fine imitation! And the author certainly seemed very comfortable writing in the genre—so much so that he penned three *Doctor Who* scripts and worked as script editor for that show for a while.

Adams visited Australia a number of times, sometimes privately, though mostly to publicise his latest work—making appearances on television and radio shows, speaking at universities and performing book-signings, as well as doing the literary luncheon/dinner circuit here.

It seems he had a soft spot for this continent. The wombat and fetid dingoes kidneys get a mention in his *Hitchhiker* books, and when it was in its early planning phase, he seriously considered hunting for the Tasmanian Tiger as part of the research for his non-fiction work co-authored with Mark Carwardine, advocating animal conservation, *Last Chance to See*.

While promoting this book, Douglas Adams delighted in telling the story of how he'd approached an Australian scientist to obtain an anti-venene kit to guard against any snake-bite emergencies he might encounter travelling in remote places around the world when researching *Last Chance to See*. "And this will keep me safe, will it?" he'd asked innocently. He relayed the answer he received from the scientist in a very broad, stereotypical Australian accent, and it was obvious that Adams enjoyed the telling all the more when speaking to a receptive Australian audience, especially when he reached the droll conclusion of the story: the kit was only effective on *Australian* snakes.

As if returning to his roots, when Douglas Adams last visited Sydney for the Sydney Writers Festival in 1998, he made a point of speaking at Sydney University. (This speech was later broadcast through Radio National and Radio Australia).

Douglas Adams is survived by his wife, Jane, and daughter, Polly, and the thousands of fans all around the world who have had their lives touched by that wholly remarkable book, *The Hitchhikers Guide to the Galaxy.*

Published in Orb *magazine, double issue 3-4, 2002. Editor: Sarah Endacott.*

The works of Douglas Adams infused a lot of my early adult life. I was a long-time member of The Hitchers Club, even serving on the committee in the club's final years. I was a member of ZZ9 Plural Z Alpha for 15 years and understand this HHG fanclub is still going strong. I also worked on a committee for a convention that Adams agreed to attend as a Guest of Honour for a short time before having to cancel due to work commitments. I was fortunate enough to see Douglas Adams at several Australian (and one British) book signings, a literary dinner in Sydney and a literary lunch in Melbourne. (I was a fan!)

**Of course, several years after this article was originally published, the* Hitchhikers Guide to the Galaxy *movie was finally released. While it only received mediocre reviews from film critics, I think, when viewed as a homage to Douglas Adams, it works.*

Keep My Things
They've Come to Take Me Home

Her Uncle Eric was somewhere between Banjo Paterson and Isaac Asimov, as at ease spinning tales about the Australian bush, where he'd spent his younger years, as he was about picturing the future.

He'd been a woodworker by trade until his retirement. After that he'd still dabbled in it as a hobby, turning out walking sticks with inspired and ornate carvings of gargoyles, dragons, or unicorn heads as handles, or a planet, with a rocket ship flying through a star field carved in relief into the stick. These he occasionally put in art shows at science fiction conventions; sometimes he sold them, but more often than not he gave them away to friends.

Uncle and niece shared a love for science fiction, though their specific tastes differed. She spent a lot of her life doing things he'd done decades before without realising she was following in his footsteps: writing her own fiction, publishing and dabbling in art.

Like him, she was incongruous: one foot in the past, one foot in the future and only one eye on the present when she really had to.

She'd been granted her own key to his terrace house years ago; it saved her having to chase after Eric if he was out and she needed access to his library for research or sanctuary. How often, in her earlier years, had she thought of herself as a female Logan, running from an early demise, escaping from the system?

The living room of the house was dimly lit, but welcoming. It smelled of old leather and gracefully aging paper. In the afternoon the sun would stream through its two tall slim windows and light that had travelled further than she ever would, caught the dust and made it dance.

A few people, some of them family, thought Eric was just a touch eccentric. They were the ones who didn't know him well. Eric kept ahead of the times when he could. He was one of the first in his circle to invest in a video player and a computer. He was accessing the internet and sending e-mail before it became a taken-for-granted part of everyday life. New technology amused and fascinated him, but it was only allowed to take up a small corner of the living room in which all the walls were devoted to shelves and all the shelves were devoted to books, pamphlets, zines, records, redundant videos and laser disks (since the players had stopped working and were beyond repair), DVDs and ephemera.

It was the books she loved most though. More often than not, if she was feeling down or upset, she would find a book that appealed to her, settle in the big leather chair underneath the windows, open up at the first page and find escape.

The leatherbound books, some dating back two centuries, were like maiden aunts sitting primly on their shelves. Occasionally she would run her fingers along their spines the way you kiss an aunt on the cheek to show affection. Sometimes she'd open them and gaze at the pages, but she'd given up trying to read them. The stories seemed too dry and brittle, like the paper they were printed on, as if the life had drained away from them through the years. She liked the more modern stuff best.

Now it felt like she was intruding, to be standing there in the midst of Eric's collection just a few days after his funeral. The living room with its floor-to-ceiling bookshelves, overflowing stacks and precarious piles, had all seemed so warm and welcoming before. Now it was just dusty and lifeless.

Hard to think of him as gone, and yet he was gone completely. No essence of him remained. This troubled her, it didn't seem right somehow. There'd been no warning; he'd been fit and well. Now she found she was angry with him for no apparent reason, and she missed him terribly.

After a while she got the feeling that she was being watched. Half expecting to see Eric in the doorway, she turned and saw Old Ken, Eric's housemate for as long as she could remember. He was a wiry old gent with grey hair and a neatly cropped beard. He stared at her with keen eyes that, even at his age, didn't miss a thing.

He always seemed around 70 years old—but she'd been thinking that about him for so long that he was probably well over 80 by now, though still fit and active. He was well-versed in a broad range of subjects and was always keen to debate anything with anyone at any time.

She recalled Friday fish suppers with Eric, Ken, and their contemporaries, where the topic of conversation would range from manned missions to Mars, intelligent life on other planets, intelligent life in present-day politicians or those of a by-gone era, and anything and everything in between.

One by one the contemporaries had died or moved away to be replaced by younger and younger faces, then not replaced at all.

"You'll sell all this I suppose?" Ken's sharp voice sliced through her reverie. Ken could tell you he was popping out to buy some milk at the local shop and make it sound like a declaration of war.

"I like science fiction too," she replied, unfazed by the apparent accusation.

She saw the look of relief in his eyes, even as he said, "But this stuff—it's not your style, is it? A lot of it written before you were born. Some of it written before *he* was born. I know he's got an early edition of Verne's in this lot somewhere." He glanced around the room and her eyes followed his.

While her Uncle Eric had been an avid collector he was no librarian. If he had a cataloguing method she'd never latched on to it.

Some of his collection was pretty rare, stories hand-written onto mimeo stencils and bearing the signatures of Heinlein or Asimov. Valuable to some, worthless to others. These days fiction and entertainment flooded the net, the reader immersed themselves in the story, the lines between book, movie, and role-playing forever blurred.

Knowing she could appreciate the rarities and oddities in his collection, Eric had left her his legacy. Many items had historical or sentimental value; the challenge was sorting them from the rest, but she'd certainly weed through his library, something she suspected Eric never thought of doing.

"I'll help you sort it out, if you want," Old Ken offered.

"I'd like that."

"Shall we make a start now?"

She'd been wanting to sit quietly with her memories and reminisce, grieve a little more, but Ken was having none of that. He strode purposefully into the living room, picked a shelf that would mark the beginning of their stock-take and carried her along in his wake. He had a code that was easy to break: anything he said "Rubbish!" to was just that and could be disposed of. For anything valuable he'd whistle through his teeth. Anything that he thought she should keep and she thought should be disposed of would be met with a few clicks of his tongue, warning her to at least think about her decision.

After a few hours of sorting, Ken suggested they break for a cup of tea.

As they sipped from cracked china cups, she gave air to the nagging feeling that had been worrying her. "You know how it feels when someone's died? You still feel some presence of them watching over you after they've gone, like they can still see you from the other side? Or maybe we just create that feeling from our memories of that person, I don't know; but I don't feel that with Eric at all. It just feels like he's gone," she confessed, expecting Old Ken to laugh at her.

Instead, Old Ken looked thoughtful and stroked his beard before answering. "We're all aliens walking on this Earth—some of us are more alien than others … it's different for us, you know!" he proclaimed, as if he'd been wanting to tell her something all along and finally she'd given him the break to do so. "For most people when you die your spirit and your body part company and your spirit goes to another place. I'm not exactly sure where, you understand—I've never been there, at least not that I can recollect."

He looked at her with much good humour and she was sure he was having a joke at her expense. "But us folk who believe in science fiction … well, we're a different animal, I reckon. We were always intended for tomorrow. So when our time is up to walk on this planet, a flying saucer arrives and two men in silver suits come to take us away."

She nearly choked on her tea trying to contain her laughter. She should have realised earlier that for people like Ken and Eric heaven was made up from the images found in pulp magazines and 'B' grade movies.

Old Ken waited until she contained her mirth before he spoke again. "Don't believe me, do you? Well then, you won't believe that's what happened with Eric when his time came. I know because I saw it, plain as day. I thought they'd come for me, you see.

Well, I had a good decade up on him, didn't I? So of course I thought I'd go before he did."

"Nice to know you've still got your imagination, Ken," she said, smiling. Of course he was trying to wind her up! She'd always suspected he shared Eric's indulgent dry humour, and she'd seen enough of him to know that he could be a ratbag when he wanted to.

"I never believed it myself when I was younger, but I've seen a few of us go that way now. Madeline, Charlie, Jock …"

She recalled faces from her uncle's old gang who used to appear at the door on Friday nights for dinner and discussion. Madeline and Ken might have had something going on for a while.

"I really look forward to my turn. There are a few authors I'll have a thing or two to tell!" Ken said in his 'off the cuff' manner.

She grinned, indulging him, then scoffed, "As if Eric would leave all his books behind! They were closer than family to him."

She had often suspected that she had run a close second, but the quest for science fiction in any of its many forms came first.

"He took one or two with him," Old Ken said, then strained more tea through his moustache. "You're doing a Mr Spock," he noted.

She was conscious of her eyebrow raised to show her scepticism. She was pretty sure Ken was baiting her. After all of these years of being a spectator to his arguments, was she finally being looked upon as a worthy opponent in a verbal jousting match? (He never argued with fools.)

"Well, I suppose it's as good an idea of the after-life as any other I've heard," she replied. But she didn't feel she was up to going three rounds with Ken on 'Was God an Astronaut, and if so, is heaven full of Little Green Men?' Instead, she drained the last of her tea and set her cup down resolutely. "Shall we get back to it?" she asked, hoping to divert Ken's attention away from a debate.

"I think I might have a nap. I'll join you again a bit later on," he told her.

He frequently took naps in the afternoon, claiming it was one of the privileges of being old. She found a certain smug comfort in knowing Ken had rest breaks. He was always trying to make out he was super-human.

He climbed the creaking stairs to his bedroom and she went back to the books.

Peace and quiet reigned for maybe an hour, then she became aware of a whirring sound, which she at first mistook for a distant alarm. It got louder and closer until finally it seemed to be right above the house, which was shaking to its foundations.

She heard Old Ken call her, so she forced herself to stand and stumble to the hallway. He was leaning over the staircase handrail, looking down at her with glee.

"There! What did I tell you?"

She'd never seen Old Ken so excited; he looked like a kid on Christmas morning.

There were bright coloured lights strobing through the windows and across the walls around the staircase and on the landing.

"It's *them*!" Old Ken yelled over the din. "Come on up if you want to see them." He retreated from her sight, probably going back into his bedroom.

Fear fought it out with curiosity, and curiosity won. She scrambled up the shaking wooden steps just in time to see Old Ken walk through his bedroom window, escorted by two humanoids in silver suits.

"Wait!" she screamed over the noise.

He turned, seemingly suspended in mid-air.

"What about your things?" she yelled, knowing his room was piled with similar memorabilia to that stacked in the living room and stored throughout the rest of the house.

He waved one decrepit book at her and called, "Keep my things—they've come to take me home!"

He winked, then turned to depart into what looked for all intents and purposes to be a large, gleaming ship that she could only describe as a flying saucer.

She was paralysed with fear, and even if she hadn't been she wouldn't have known what to do. With a high-pitched whine that stopped abruptly the ship was gone, leaving her dumbfounded. When her wits returned, she bolted from the house and stood in the street looking skyward—drawing curious glances from those who passed around her, seemingly untouched by the extraordinary event.

There was no sign of the flying saucer, no sign of damage to the old house. The way it had been shaking she had at least expected to see cracks, but there was no hint that anything remotely unusual had occurred.

If that old bastard has laced my tea with psychotropic drugs, so help me, I'm going to ... she thought as she climbed the front stairs. But then she remembered they'd shared the same teapot.

The stairs up to the first floor creaked, but moved no more than usual as she climbed them, sure she'd find Old Ken asleep on his bed. He wasn't there, which only served to raise her fears of being accused of his murder. Who should she contact? There wasn't a body, so how could she contact a doctor or the police? Family? She wasn't even sure if Ken had any family. But someone would miss him sooner or later ... she was the last to see him ... how was anyone going to believe *this*? She felt cold and sick. Where had she left her sanity?

And it all went rushing around in her mind over and over again, like a pack of greyhounds chasing a lure, getting nowhere.

She struggled with her delusional state to answer a knock at the door, half-expecting to be confronted by two humanoids wearing silver space suits telling her it was *her* time to go. She crept to the door and opened it cautiously.

A man in a dark suit and sunglasses smiled at her.

"I'm Charles Starr from Starr Funerals. I have reason to believe you're in need of our services …?"

He presented his business card to her in a flourish. "May I come in?"

Stunned, she opened the door to him and he found his way to the kitchen. Slowly and methodically he explained it all to her, patiently repeating the facts until her numb brain was able to absorb them and she came to understand the essence of the subterfuge: a weighted coffin, a simple service, and no one any the wiser … except maybe a few like her who came to know. The invitation to travel among the stars was rarely refused by those who were called.

She still didn't believe it, but he didn't seem to expect her to, merely to accept that she had nothing to worry about and that he'd take care of everything. She reciprocated his professional pleasantness as she saw him to the door.

But anger rose within her as she returned to the livingroom lined with books. "If I *ever* catch up with Ken or Eric again, so help me I'll show them what for!" she seethed. But now, much to her surprise, she felt she *would* catch up with them again sometime in the future, and she looked forward to that day.

'Keep My Things They've Come to Take Me Home' was published in Fables and Reflections, *Issue 2, 2002. Editor: Lily Chrywenstrom.*

You may have noticed the title owes itself to a line in Peter Gabriel's song, 'Solsbury Hill'.

This story is a fanciful look at how science fiction fans may solve the problem of mortality in their own unique way. It was written as a reaction to the death of a friend and of a relative in quick succession. There's also a bit of a nod to Sydney SF fan, Kevin Dillon. I never saw his house, but I've heard the stories of his hoard of books and magazines.

When Whales Cry

The two of us stand by the rail on the starboard side of the ice-breaker. We're cocooned in thermal layers against the freezing cold that is an Antarctic summer. Squinting, we look across the waves for that elusive thing that brought us together.

He gratefully accepts the ginger-extract travel-sickness tablet I offer him. To say that he looks green around the gills is an understatement.

Funny, but I thought I was going to be the one to get sea-sick, not this Scientist with the youthful face and the heart of an angel.

With a swig of bottled water, he swallows the tablet.

I consider the absurdity of his action. Here we are, surrounded by icebergs of pristine white and untouched purity, and he's drinking bottled water brought with us from Hobart.

"Thar she blows!" cries one of the crewmen from the crow's-nest, who delights in playing at 'Down to the Sea in Ships'. I wish he wouldn't. A simple "Whale sighted" would suit me fine.

I glance at the Scientist. He still looks sick, but with grim determination he pushes himself away from the railing. He knows we have a job to do.

The ship rolls slightly as we change our direction to get closer to the whale we've spotted. Only one whale. I'd been hoping to encounter large pods to make our work more effective, but the big pods—if such things exist anymore—have eluded us so far.

Some times when we're lucky we see pairs and trios of whales. Mostly though it's individuals. Up in the tropics I'm told they used to mingle in large numbers, meeting to breed and birth their young, but large groupings have become rare even there. Have we finally taught them not to congregate in numbers? Or are there just so few of them remaining? Yet we still hunt them.

Further up the deck some of the crew prepare to lower a rubber inflatable boat into the ocean swell.

"You don't have to do it, you know," I tell the Scientist. "I've watched you enough. I could probably do it this time, if you prefer?"

He swallows back his nausea and says, "No, I'll be fine."

Stubborn bastard, but I guess I like that about him. Like me, he has to do things his way. Like me, his chosen profession will never be just a career to him—a well-paid, slick rise to fame and the respect of his peers. His heart is too big for that, near to bursting with an overwhelming need to change the world, and I can relate to that too.

Awkwardly but carefully we all board the small boat. We are jostled around as the rubber dinghy parts company with the ship, caught in the swell before it heads out across the choppy blue-grey waves to where a darker grey fin is oblivious to keeping a date with destiny.

"Make it easy for us," I pray silently to the whale. "Make it easy on yourself. We do what we have to do."

What it lacks in stability, the small inflatable boat makes up for in speed. Yet we have to take care as we bounce over the waves. If we tipped into the whale's domain, it would be the water's cold, not the whale, that killed us. Even the chill of the air transcends cold and becomes pain. Daggers of ice cold air chisel at our exposed faces.

Busy concentrating on shallow diving, the whale seems unperturbed by the irritating buzzing of our outboard motor. The pilot cuts back the throttle and we glide silently towards the leviathan.

The Scientist removes his gloves, takes the rifle from the floor of the boat, sets an arching grey back in his sights, and fires.

Our harpoon finds its mark. A small barbed arrow at the end of a long hollow needle which in turn is attached to a vial. A miniature harpoon. Not my choice of shape for a weapon, but an effective necessity. The barb keeps the needle in place long enough for a microchip and the contents of the vial to be pumped into the whale's blubber. Within an hour the barb will work loose. The small wound will heal over, with only a small white cross of scar tissue as the symbol that this whale has been anointed. If we come across this whale again in our travels, the microchip will alert us that we have already visited this individual and we will let it go along its way.

The sensitive whale skin quivers in a movement similar to the tremor of a horse's flank trying to shift an irksome fly. With a flick of its massive tail that barely disturbs the surface of the ocean, the whale dives a little deeper and swims away.

The Scientist puts down his gun. His complexion looks healthier for the chase. His cheeks are made ruddy from the cold breeze, and his eyes are bright. I, by comparison, must look distressed because he reaches across to me. With his bare hand he squeezes me firmly through my thick gloves, encouraging my courage, my hope.

"A mosquito's bite, nothing more," he promises me, then lets his hands find the warm confines of his own gloves.

"That's our twenty-fourth minke whale," the pilot records. He aims a remote sensor in the direction of the departing whale and it pings. Satisfied that the microchip is secure, he navigates the rubber dinghy back to nestle by the ship where it will latch on to a metal nub in an imitation of a whale calf suckling at its mother's nipple.

No rich milk will be squirted down our throats, but a nip of celebratory whisky (I hate the stuff!) with the captain awaits us on the bridge when we're safely back on board. It's a tradition the captain initiated for this momentous voyage.

The Scientist always drinks his ration no matter how sea-sick he feels. Quite often he helps me finish mine. He looks triumphant, but I don't feel triumphant yet. It concerns me that we've sighted so few whales. Not for the first time I worry. How few are left? Masters of their domain once, they travelled all the oceans of the world in their thousands, filling the depths with their calls. Now the seas are mostly silent, the rare whalesong a mournful lament of happier days long since gone. Have I left my ambitions too late?

I'd inherited my father's share and property portfolio three years ago. A little careful planning, a few near-reckless gambles that paid off, have catapulted me from being a mere mortal with enough money to live comfortably on to being mega-rich. I had always longed for money and now that I have it in great abundance, I know just how to spend it.

The Scientist wasn't that hard to find. His image was plastered across the covers of *New Scientist*, *Newsweek*, and *Time*. He was the Face of the Year a few years back. He was the one who'd developed the virus that causes African elephants to shed their tusks every four years, much in the same way that deer lose their antlers. During the time their tusks are growing the animals are infertile, which keeps their numbers under control.

It's far less dangerous to collect ivory off the ground than to stalk and kill a wild elephant, and by re-growing tusks, the elephant becomes a welcome resource that can be regularly harvested rather than a competitor for land and vegetation. It was a win/win situation. And that's the only reason African elephants aren't extinct now.

When his 15 minutes of fame was over, when he dropped gratefully back into obscurity, I paid the Scientist to work for me, to develop that missing link I needed for my dream project to come true. He worked for me willingly, keen to meet the challenge I had set him; partly to satisfy his own curiosity, partly because he believed in my cause. Officially he's working on something else entirely. But then officially none of us are here. At this moment, I'm on the ski fields of Klosters, and have at least six friends who will testify that I was in their company there if anyone should ask. I've even got the holiday snaps to prove it too.

Securing the use of the ship we're on wasn't as hard as I'd thought it'd be. Even if I didn't have the money to pay for their services, I suspect the captain and the crew—even the fledgling Captain Ahab up in the crow's-nest—would have joined me on my mission.

We're all like-minded individuals. We all supported Greenpeace and the conservationists, and thought the tide had turned, our battle won, when whale watching replaced whale hunting along so many shorelines. We all watched the political manipulating and the vote-buying that went on in the International Whaling Commission in order to get commercial whaling back on the agenda. We can all see the way the world is heading, and have all tired of shouting "Stop!"

But even though people listen, the ones in power—in parliaments and committees all over the world—never want to hear. Words of protest, of disgust and outrage, don't achieve the results I'm seeking.

I decided silence was better than shouting.

There aren't many who know I'm spending the Australian summer in Antarctica, consoling a sea-sick Scientist and harpooning whales with miniature spears which are just as deadly as their full-size semblances, but not to the whales.

With my support, the Scientist has created another virus. That's what we're injecting the whales with. Virulent enough to spread from whale to whale whenever their skins touch (and like us humans, they are sensual, tactile creatures). Whenever they share the lightest caress, or make love; whenever the young suckle from their mothers, and even when their spouting breaths intermingle, the virus will leap between them, spreading quickly and quietly, infiltrating all parts of each massive body, yet causing no harm to the host—nor even to the natural predators of the cetaceans. Planted like a silent time bomb, the virus will lurk inside every whale waiting to rid the ocean of the plague of unnatural hunters.

This whaling season, or maybe next, the news broadcasts will be filled with tales of a deadly new disease that only affects those who have consumed whale meat. With any luck they'll blame mercury poisoning, or something similar. The world's oceans are polluted enough to produce scores of potential suspects: chemical run off, dumping, the wrecks of nuclear submarines. Will anyone even bother to look any further? Will anyone even suspect? But the market for whale meat will collapse. Then they'll stop hunting the cetaceans. Forever.

We have tried fighting with words, but words were never enough. Only my words have found an obscure path to the goal so many of us tried to achieve: to make the killing stop once and for all. No more moratoria, no more transparent excuses about killing whales for "scientific research". This time we fight science with science.

The Scientist looks well. Either my travel-sickness tablet has worked, or his pride in his achievement keeps his mind off the rise and fall of the ship as he scans the horizon.

The ship rolls slightly in the swell as we creep stealthily between icebergs, looking for another grey back to anoint.

'When Whales Cry' was written as a reaction to a TV documentary about whaling, compered by Olivia Newton John, which I just happened to catch when I was flicking through channels one summer. I'm a self-confessed 'Whale Geek', having pursued a layman's interest in cetaceans for many years now. It's no surprise that my first published novel was The Whale's Tale *featuring a humpback whale, a bottlenose dolphin and a teenage Japanese girl all travelling together on a massive spaceship that has an Inner Ocean at its core.*

I liked this Scientist guy so much, I went back and wrote him into a prequel using the same two main characters called 'Never Forget'.

'When Whales Cry' was published in Potato Monkey, *Issue 3, Winter 2003. Editor: Ben Payne. It also appears as a bonus story in e-copies of my YA SF novel,* The Whale's Tale.

We Were A Family Then

The latching of a wire screen door,
Puts me in mind of a time
Years before,
When it was fresh,
And newly painted.
We were a family then.

The cracks of their age
Just beginning to show,
Into the car,
To the Highlands we'd go.
They in their dotage,
And me in my prime.
We were a family then.

They speak the truth,
When they say "Time flies".
My 'Younger Than Springtime' has long since died.
And that sad wizened old man in the hospital bed,
It's hard to recall him before his health fled.
And now even I view my future with dread.
But we were a family then.

Published in The Mozzie *(aka* Micropress Oz*) Vol 10, Issue 5, June 2002. Editor: Gloria B. Yates.*

Writes of Passage

"If you were going to be a writer it would have happened by now," my mother told me once, years ago.

Cruel words meant to be kind, meant to show her daughter, her only child, that you don't always get the things you want in life.

She was my mother, my friend, my confidant. Of course she was right.

My life flowed in other directions. I learned different skills, learned more about myself. I grew.

Believing the childhood fairy stories, I waited for love to come and sweep me off my feet. I always thought, like everyone else, I'd get married and leave home some day. There were a few chances, but none of them felt right. No regrets. I stayed at home with Mum.

At some stage the role between us altered, swapped. I became the nurturer, advice-giver, teacher, while she became the dependent child. "Get me this while you're out." "Drive me here." "Now, this weekend I've planned for us ..."

Her shrewdness and ability to manipulate my life, to get her own way, annoyed me at times. But she was my Mum, and I loved her. And hadn't she given me that same attention when I was younger? Fair's fair. Besides, we were friends, and friends curve and sway to accommodate each other.

I wasn't completely dependent. I had my own friends and interests too, you understand. Yet she was such an integral part of my life, such a constant, reassuring thing. I thought there'd be nothing for me to live for when she died. The concept of being without her terrified me.

But no one lives forever.

She died one night after a ten-day illness that got me used to the fact that maybe it was her time to go. I thought my world would end with her demise.

The sun came up the next morning, none the wiser that my life had changed. The world went on around me while I mourned my loss. Friends supported me with their love, surrounded me with their understanding while I grieved.

My mother's death was the one single thing in my life I thought I'd never be able to cope with. I thought its impact would crush me completely. But I got by. I learned to adjust to the changes that washed over me.

At first it felt strange having my spare time entirely to myself. Strange and lonely, because there wasn't that slow, old presence by my side any more, holding me back, making me wait. I learned to walk at my own pace, learned to do what I wanted to do when I wanted to do it.

Who'd have thought that independence could be such a frightening thing? So liberating, yet so daunting? Where was that wise old soul I used to speak freely with? She was no more. I was left with vacant white sheets of paper waiting to hear what I told them by word and pen. They listened carefully, but gave no answer. All the answers were in myself now.

I survived my mother's death. I've faced my greatest fear and come through the other side not unscathed, but stronger, better. No longer afraid of who I am and what I want to be.

In the days my mother hovered, trying to decide between life and death, I took to writing again. I poured my emotions into written words because they had to go somewhere. They kept welling up inside me, and I would only have flooded my friends with them if they'd been spoken. Often, I'd be writing 'blind' because I couldn't see the paper in front of me through my tears. But the words knew where to fall.

I wrote my heart out in a journal.

I've held that journal in my hands a number of times, but never dared open it to read more than a few sentences. When I do, the memories all come washing back and I start to cry again.

But I remembered the solace writing used to offer a lonely girl all those years ago. Slowly, I've come back to enjoy the freedom and the discipline of putting pen to paper, fingers to keyboard; of expressing myself in written words.

Some flowers bloom later than others, I tell myself. Some flowers never bloom at all, but I press on regardless.

I don't set myself a "sell by" date. I'm never going to tell myself, "Well, it should have happened by now." If it doesn't happen at all, if no one acknowledges me for what I see myself to be, at least I acknowledge to myself that I'm a writer with every single sentence I create.

So maybe Mum was wrong. Or maybe, with a thicker hide, I'm not prepared to accept she might be right. All I know is that I survived my mother's death. After that, I've got the strength to face anything.

Written in 1997.

Biography in a Tea Cup

Take one confused, lonely child; someone who was always made to feel that little bit different, not quite the same. An Outsider. Now stir. Let her find her way into writing, let her think that she's got a gift, she's got a talent, that she can change her entire world with just a few strokes of her pen. Well, she does that. She writes about living on other planets, living in castles and talking to common and magical creatures alike, who naturally talk back.

Engaged by her own ingenuity, writing to get away, without knowing what she's getting away from. It would take years before she discovered there are countless others out there, also confused, misunderstood and lonely, also needing to escape. Always have been, always will be. (And she thought she was the only one.) There's no such thing as special, yet everyone is unique. While we might all write about similar subjects, we each live in our individual minds and write with our own distinct style.

I started out with nothing when I decided I wanted to be a writer. After all these years, I still have half of it left. (Paraphrasing Groucho Marx here, but I'm sure he wouldn't mind. The title of my collection also owes itself to a line from a Marx Brothers movie.)

I've just blown the dust off an award I won for a writing competition held forty years ago. Annual awards were offered by a science fiction club I belonged to. Some of my earliest writing was published in science fiction fanzines. You can still see their influence in some of my work, though apparently that's not how you write *proper* science fiction or fantasy (a statement that has since been proven false by a number of best-selling books that crossed the streams.) I'm not going to apologise for some of my more fannish-inspired work. Writing for fanzines helped make me the writer that I am today. I should have been grateful then for the opportunity to use my imagination and learn my craft (and there's still so much to learn), but I was young, driven and egocentric. I'm grateful now.

After a few false starts ("We'll publish your story in our next issue! Oops, sorry, we're closing the magazine instead.") and a lot of rejection letters (which haven't really stopped, but I've found they're best treated with chocolate, purely for medicinal purposes), I finally started getting stories published in SF magazines and anthologies.

My first (still unpublished) novel was a YA SF/Romance titled *Boyfriend Wanted: No Experience Necessary.* It was shortlisted in the inaugural George Turner Prize offered by Transworld Publishers in 1998. It went on to be placed in the top 20% of its category in the Emma Darcy Awards for Romantic Fiction in the same year. I have won the ASFMA Award for writing twice, and won the Australian Science Fiction Foundation (Ditmar) Awards for best fan editor (with my colleague, Ted Scribner) three times for producing the web, print and email newsletter, a revivified edition of The Australian Science Fiction Bullsheet. I've received Honourable Mentions in the Mary Grant Bruce Awards twice.

My YA Science fiction novel, *The Whale's Tale*, was published in 2009. A collection of interlinked urban/rural fantasy stories called *The Back of the Back of Beyond* was published in 2013.

I was also one of the founding members of the Andromeda Spaceways Inflight Magazine Publishing Co-op, which reengaged my passion for editing. Having gained professional editing qualifications, I now work as a freelance editor, encouraging other writers.

Like my writing, my CV is a little scattered. If I was a race-horse, you'd bet on me for a place rather than a win, but I'm still here, and I'm still writing. I haven't been sent to the glue factory yet.

Why not check out the other books in the Peggy Bright
Books catalogue?
All books are available in paperback, and in various e-book
formats (pdf, epub, and mobi), direct from our website.

Peggy Bright Books

www.peggybrightbooks.com

Also by Edwina Harvey

The Whale's Tale

A Young Adult SF novel

Uki is a teenage Japanese girl caught stealing a file from a spacefaring whale, Targe, to impress a guy in her gang. She has to perform restitution to Targe by touring the Galaxy with him and his dolphin sidekick, Charlie. Uki doesn't like Targe, Targe doesn't like Uki, and Charlie thinks he's in for the worst tour of his life until they discover Uki has a special talent.

ISBN 9780980699807

Also by Edwina Harvey

The Back Of The Back Of Beyond

A collection of interlinked short stories

Be introduced to an Australian landscape you never knew existed, somewhere out in the back of the back of beyond, where it matters whether there's room to park a dragon, and where 'the next door neighbours' on a rural backblock are out of this world, but the parties are legendary.

ISBN 9780980699869

Also available from Peggy Bright Books

LIGHT TOUCH PAPER, STAND CLEAR

Matchless prose to fire your imagination

Edited by Edwina Harvey and Simon Petrie

Short speculative fiction from Jo Anderton, Brenda Cooper, Thoraiya Dyer, Dave Luckett, Sean McMullen, and other award-winning Australian and international authors.

ISBN 9780980699821

USE ONLY AS DIRECTED

A varied mix of speculative fiction stories

Edited by Simon Petrie and Edwina Harvey

New stories from Stephen Dedman, Dirk Flinthart, Dave Freer, Lyn McConchie, Charlotte Nash, Janeen Webb, and others.

ISBN 9780980699876

THE TAME ANIMALS OF SATURN

A compendium of fantastical animals

by Adam Browne

A sumptuously-illustrated surrealistic adventure inspired by the extraterrestrial menagerie of nineteenth-century Christian mystic Jakob Lorber.

ISBN 9780980699890